A Pa

Obse

A Patient Obsession

A NOVEL

Meryl Dunton-Rose

North Bank

North Bank Institute of Independent Studies
PO Box 153, Bellingen, NSW, 2454, Australia
lizardland@bigpond.com

A Patient Obsession
2021

ISBN 978-0-9757636-4-3

 A catalogue record for this
work is available from the
National Library of Australia

A Patient Obsession, a novel
Author: Meryl Dunton-Rose
Cover photograph: Meryl Dunton-Rose
Cover design: Ross Macleay

For my sister

and mine!

with much love,

xx

February 2022

Patient: Having or exercising patience (with, to, or towards a person, fault etc.)

Obsession: (The action of) an idea or image which continually or persistently fills the mind

Shorter Oxford English Dictionary

Preface

As with all good stories this one is influenced by real-life events. I must hasten to add that it is, indeed, fiction.

Having discovered some letters written by my mother I wove my story around them. I must admit as I end this story, I find myself now unable to discern the fact from the fiction.

When you read about Henry and Patience consider the sadness of an obsession. What do you do when a reality does not live up to the dream?

Prologue

July 2001
San Cassiano, Tuscany

The wooden shelter feels rough on my skin. I need the abrasion. It reminds me of why I am here; it tears into my skin, splinters reaching for my heart and my soul.

My father's obsession sits: a crumpled, faded old lady on the bench. She gazes into the valley, misty as her eyes. The smooth brown skin of her hands strokes the container in her lap. It doesn't even have the dignity of an urn. A blue plastic box with a sticker on the end of it; what a banal repository for the cremated remains of one's loved one. She doesn't even look at me as she slowly stands up, walks towards the plunging hillside into the valley, hesitates as I take in an alarmed breath; but before I can dart forward she pops open the top and flings the ashes. They float and dance on the shimmering portal of the void. The last of them fall at her feet, covering her shins in a soft grey film. I hear the faint patter of a bone making its way down amongst the thyme and the rocks.

Thyme and time.

Part 1

Chapter 1

The black wrought iron letters he had so often seen in his mind were now solid against the stone wall. Henry paused, hammer in mid-air, and stepped back to view the nameplate. *Casa Pazienza.* Henry liked the way the rounded C sheltered the rest of the word as if enclosing the house in its embrace. He liked the motherly shape of the capital P. He hammered home the last of the nails and looked at his watch as the hot sun rose above dusty trees illuminating the courtyard, bathing the stones, turning them a deeper gold. He made his way up the stone steps hollowed out by generations of feet, and grimaced slightly at the pain coursing down his left leg. He fumbled in the inside gloom; his fingers searched for the keys he was convinced he had placed on the marble side table in the entrance hall. He righted the photo frame he had knocked over, running his hand lovingly over the portrayed figure. He lifted it closer, ever closer, until he could see the seam of her stocking, the shine on her leather belt. The scent of the jasmine planted outside the front door caused him to blink. Not the same perfume at all; no, not at all.

His eyes refocused, he glanced in the mirror, dusted a stray piece of fluff off his left shoulder, half-smiled at images he had never forgotten, and left the house. At every bend of the familiar mountain road, trees brushed memories, smoothed their edges and polished them to perfection. The breeze sneaking through the open car window caressed his cheek; he can see her hair so dark, curls unkempt, blown by the wind as she sits beside him in his father's pride and joy, the red Singer Lemans he had begged to borrow, the long bonnet polished so vigorously earlier in the day as thanks. Laughing, she turns and shouts to Max and Elsie in the back seat. Knees folded, gripping the seats, they strain to hear what she is saying. She laughs again, shrugs her shoulders and grins at Henry. His glance slips from the road ahead to her olive-skinned hand tucking curls behind her ear.

April 1947
Rhyl, North Wales

It was a Tuesday. He had taken to walking behind her on the way to the post office. Familiar with the route she took, he lounged, casually smoking, against a telegraph pole, willing her to look at him. It was her skin, he thought, wonderfully soft, creamy brown, luminescent, reflecting colours, absorbing them as its own; her blue-black hair and her smile. Perfect. No, not perfect; her two front teeth slightly overlapped. Shiny red shoes with peep toes that he would later see on her slim feet held her gaze as she passed Miranda's shoe shop window. He followed a few paces behind and waited outside the post office. Tomorrow, he thought, he would bring a letter, stand behind her in the queue, and breathe in the floral fragrance she left in her wake, an unusual mix of jasmine and frangipani.

On Wednesday Henry grasped a letter in his hand and followed her on her usual route towards the post office. She stopped suddenly, almost causing him to collide with her, a collision he had not planned for. He dropped quickly to one knee retying a shoelace, staring at his home address on the envelope. He would have to visit soon. He rose and followed as she continued walking down Mount Street and around the corner where the newspaper vendor stood. She waved a neatly manicured hand in greeting.

"Lovely day!" the vendor said as he smiled back at her.

Closer; Henry wanted to get closer, to hear the words coming from her red lips. Words he wanted to collect, put into his pocket and take out to cherish over and over again. He would not cast them aside or utter a banality like the newspaper vendor.

It was Thursday when her red peep-toed footsteps rang out on the tarmacadam; he could hear them, neater, surely purer than those of the crowd surrounding her. Henry stood behind her in the queue. How could she not feel him behind her? His every taut nerve twanged with the tension. She smoothed her skirt and admired her shoes. His eyes followed hers – if only she would turn and look at him. As she was called to the counter he breathed again, realising that his chest had been squeezed tight behind his polished buttons. It was his turn to buy a stamp from another smiling post office worker, to lick the stamp and send the letter. Thanking the clerk, he spun on his shiny military heel and hurried out after the girl. He could see her receding, her houndstooth jacket cinched tightly at the waist. Where was she going? She should have turned left onto Broad Street and back to the bank. Apologising to an elderly mauve lady in his way, he sidestepped her disobedient shopping trolley. Halfway down the street, the girl stopped and peered into a window. He watched as she ran her tongue over her teeth, baring them to check for lipstick traces. Running her fingers through her wayward dark curls, she cajoled them into place and stepped away from her reflection.

Her pace slowed, he stopped and appeared interested in golden, milk-shined pasties in a bakery window, watched flies lazily land on scones imitating the raisins until they rubbed their legs together. Out of the corner of his eye, he watched her turn into a small bow-fronted teashop. She ducked her head under the low doorframe, and he heard the tinkle of the bell attached to the back of the door. He saw her distorted image through the mottled glass panes make its way to a small round table in the corner. He hesitated as he walked past, deciding whether to go in or whether the confined space would restrict him, oblige him to acknowledge her.

He gasped as he saw the uniformed male figure seated opposite her. His heart beat faster; he tried to loosen his collar. Anguish coursed through his veins. She was smiling coquettishly; or was it a grimace? As he stared, the distorted glass in the old windowpane caused her image to flicker between one and the other. He turned briskly and walked on a few paces before abruptly turning around. A small boy yelped as his nose hit Henry's knee.

"Mind where you're going!" his angry mother threw at Henry's rapidly retreating back.

Henry decided to enter the teashop and sat at a table in the window, the furthest table away from the couple engrossed in each other. American, he thought, that would be right. They come and take all the prettiest girls. He studied the menu and told the waitress to bring him a cup of tea and a Chelsea bun. He was conscious that he had nothing to hide behind and tried to stare out at the street. An old man stuttered past leaning on a stick; two boys with peaked school caps raced by with satchels banging against their backs; an officer he vaguely knew stopped and looked into the café and briefly saluted him. He hoped he wasn't going to come in for tea or coffee; he was not in the mood for conversation with an acquaintance. He would prefer to eavesdrop on the girl and her companion.

He strained to hear the outline of their words: murmurings punctuated by laughter. He dared not turn his head. He turned over the menu and brushed away a few stray crumbs. A petal dropped from a faded pink dog rose in a tarnished vase. The waitress brought him his tea, slopped into its saucer, and a bun that looked as though the flies in the bakery window had been visiting.

Glowing words "Saturday dance", "meet at seven o'clock" burnt themselves onto his brain. The table became too hot to touch. His breath rasped as he pushed the seat back, stood up and left, almost at a run. If he had glanced back, he would have seen all the diners looking with curiosity at his uneaten bun, barely sipped tea and a florin thrown carelessly on the table. Two old ladies interrupted their scones and jam to shake their jowls and 'tut tut' as the door slammed behind him.

He strode toward the seafront, overtook the strollers on the promenade and headed along the pier, heedless of the dropped ice cream and pieces of candyfloss. Oblivious to the shrieks from the Sticky Fly as it whirled around dropping the bottom out of other people's worlds, he continued to the end of the pier. The tide was high. Henry was surprised to look down and see salt spray on his boots, his grey-blue trousers flecked with foam brought in on the sea breeze. His finely chiselled features were as grey as the Irish Sea relentlessly pounding the pebbles. The breakwaters glistened.

After a time, his pacing slowed, and his heart stopped pounding. As he walked more slowly back to the boarding house, he began to take note of his surroundings. A couple with arms encircling each other's waists, eyes gazing at each other, elicited a wry smile from him. He stopped to pat a small fluffy dog who waddled beside a small fluffy lady. Both were wearing red woollen jackets, silver buttons bulging, and he laughed at the absurdity of it all.

Tall lime-washed, pebble-dashed houses sported 'No Vacancy' signs. Reaching a tidy grey house with clean – if flaky – white wood trim, he took the steps two at a time, noticing that the curtains were not yet pulled. A meagre electric bar glowed in the living room giving the brown leather chairs a strange, almost incandescent quality. He wiped his shoes energetically and followed the dingy patterned carpet to his room. He noted with satisfaction the accuracy of the placement of the brass number five, exactly in the middle of the centre panel of the door. Warming the metal with his breath he took out his handkerchief and polished off a fingerprint.

Henry unlocked the door and shut it quietly behind him. He took off his jacket, hung it on the wooden hanger left behind the door and placed his cap on the dressing table. A look of distaste passed over his face as he flicked a brown hair out of the sink. He washed his hands, humming the happy birthday song for the requisite twenty seconds as his nanny had taught him, and wiped them with care on the small once-white towel folded across the metal bracket under the sink. He replaced the towel and evened its ends. He sat on the bed and picked up the book on his bedside table, but barely glanced at it before he laid it down on the candlewick bedspread. His hand rested on the cover and obscured the title. He stared unseeingly at the floral wallpaper. Gradually his scrambled thoughts ordered themselves firmly in serried ranks. The dinner bell tinkled downstairs. He tugged a jumper over his head, smoothed his ruffled hair and as he left his room, he checked that the latch was pushed up to lock his bedroom door.

The stair runners clicked as he made his way down to the dining room. Although he was careful not to hit his head on the door lintel, Henry straightened up immediately he entered the room, needing every inch of advantage when confronting Mrs Richards, the landlady. She presided at the head of the table, her hands spread out on either side of her plate. After a perfunctory greeting to those present, Captain Henry Parker sat down. The smell of boiled cabbage reminded him of boarding school lunches. He started to think instead about coriander and cumin, ground fenugreek and fennel; it made the food more palatable as he did so, whilst greatly missing the crisp pakoras and creamy saag panir that he so loved.

Mrs Richards felt it her duty to ask each of her lodgers how they had spent the day. She paused when her gaze arrived at an empty seat around the table. Her disapproval of latecomers was obvious through her querulous tone.

Henry stepped in.

"I spent most of the time along the promenade. I had a very pleasant tea at Hussey's on William Street. Do you know of it?" Henry proffered smoothly.

A flurry of apology and trailing scarves tripped into the room. Henry was spared any further inquisition as Mrs Richards turned her basilisk gaze on the latecomer, Miss Hughes, whose transgression was rewarded with cold cabbage and lukewarm mutton stew. Funny, he thought, mannerisms must be bred into generations. His mother used to spread her fingers angrily just like Mrs Richards was doing. He remembered his mother at the dinner table, her rings impatiently changing colours in the light revealing far more than her demeanour ever would. He remembered standing at the door in anguish, his garbled explanations of playing in the copse, trying to build a treehouse and having stick fights being met with frosty disdain. His elder sister would sit, smirking. He would wriggle into his seat leaving a trail of leafy debris, swept up later by a disapproving housekeeper. His mother resonated haughtiness throughout the meal, her cutlery clinking impatiently on the china plate. She would barely meet his father's eye which had managed to throw a surreptitious wink in Henry's direction.

The clattering of plates being cleared brought to Henry's attention Miss Hughes' discomfort as it radiated in throbbing, painful waves. Mrs Richards blushed at her rudeness and flashed a compensatory smile at Miss Hughes.

"I managed to get some custard powder today, so we have some syrup pudding as a treat." She gathered up the plates noisily and swept out of the room. Nervous murmurings erupted into conversation, conversations he wished to have no part of; and excusing himself from the promised dessert, he took himself back to his room to prepare himself for the morrow.

Chapter 2

April 1947

He had practised his patter in front of the mirror. Shiny phrases like rounded coins jumped into his mouth; he swallowed them down and they bumped and jingled in his stomach as his feet resolutely took themselves towards the brightly-lit hotel which shone like the moon at the end of the street. Despite all his mental preparation he still felt lacking in courage.

The heavy mahogany doors swung open so suddenly that he had to step back to avoid being hit in the chest by shiny brass handles. Two servicemen in the blue uniform of the Americans dragged on their cigarettes, eyes squinting to avoid the curling smoke. One of them drawled a "Sorry there, buddy," and tapped down the hotel steps.

The scene meeting his eyes shattered into a thousand fragments as the mirrored ball twirled in the centre of the ceiling above the dancing couples. Laughter, music, tight-waisted dresses. Bright red lipstick on open mouths. Shiny smooth hair glinted the colour of horse chestnuts. So many blue uniforms, such a swirl of colours, shreds of fabric disassembled and reassembled into whirling partners.

Henry's breathing was shallow. His heart raced as he glanced towards the bar. Blond hair, dark hair, neatly rolled and held in place by pins and combs. There. He spotted the ebony curls, darkly picking up reflections from the mauve of her silk dress. A black belt encircled her waist. Trim calves were longitudinally divided by the seams of her stockings. His eye followed down to agitated feet as they tapped to the beat.

Henry began to walk forward, swallowing frequently, shaping a smile, straightening an already straight jacket. She turned and laughed in his direction, whispered into the ear of her shorter friend whose pale pink jacket was eclipsed by the rustling purple silk of her dress. Before Henry could say a word the two girls gave a coy wave to the soldiers they had been talking to and headed off towards the ladies' room. The men smiled conspiratorially and took long swigs from their glasses. Henry ordered a pint from the barman and leant against the bar. Why had he thought he could do this? He didn't trust himself. He turned his back to the girls as they returned.

"Here, Patience, I got you a Pimms, whatever that is," drawled the taller of the two soldiers. Henry smiled. Patience. Now he knew her name. Now he could approach her directly.

"And I got one for you too, Elsie," said the other.

Slowly Henry turned around and faced Patience. She did not look at him; her gaze was firmly directed at the tall soldier bending down toward her, smiling into her face, his hand placed on the small of her back. Henry stared at the soft down of her face which encased it like glowing dust, smudging the outline of her features. He longed to run his fingertip along her jaw to the small delicate earlobe, to continue tracing the contours of her ear, to smooth her lively eyebrows. The girl in pink stood on tiptoe and whispered something in Patience's ear. Her glance flickered toward him but did not rest. She appeared to be looking over his left shoulder at someone or something before she switched her gaze directly at him. Her voice was clear above the laughter and the surrounding conversation.

"Oh, him. He's the one I told you about. The one who's been following me. I wish he'd leave me alone."

Henry picked up his beer and studied the froth. He thought he had been unobtrusive in trying to find out her name and who she was, but she had noticed him. Enough to recognise him. Perhaps she'd seen his face when he bent down to tie his shoes? Why hadn't she acknowledged him? How many times had he followed her? He couldn't recall. It was ten days since he had come home on leave. Maybe a dozen times? The first sweat needled under his collar. He wiped his upper lip with his handkerchief. Turned around once more.

Patience was no longer looking at him but was staring up at the GI who had again put his arm around her waist and was pulling her towards him. Patience held a curl between her thumb and forefinger and stretched it down over one eye as she looked up at him through her lashes with a practised smile. The soldier pressed her to him tightly. Her smile faltered; she squirmed a little and stepped back.

"How about another drink? I think it's your round, Jack."

Jack shrugged but caught his friend's gesture as he tipped up an imaginary glass.

"I guess so. Same again for you, Patience? I'll get the bartender to make a cocktail we have back home for you, Elsie."

"Oh, no. I couldn't; I can't drink any more."

"Sure you can! This one will taste like pop, believe me."

Elsie giggled as she took the drink out of Jack's hand. She sipped tentatively.

"How d'you like it? It's called a whisky sour."

"Whisky! I can't drink that."

"Sure you can; just like your lemonade with a kick," he laughed.

Elsie tugged at Patience's elbow,

"I don't want to drink, I want to dance."

"Well, down the hatch then and we'll dance." She tipped the glass up and Henry watched her throat as she swallowed. She licked her lips like a greedy child and called out over her shoulder as she grasped Elsie's hand and pulled her onto the dance floor.

"Jack, Tom, come on! It's my favourite dance tune."

Henry caught glimpses of the pale pink, the swirling lilac, receding and advancing, a kaleidoscope of shifting patterns. He pressed his forefingers to his temples and rotated them whilst narrowing his eyes. The giddiness passed but the chatter and the noise still made him feel light-headed. He stayed a few minutes more but unable to spot Patience in the swirling melee he turned on his heel and left the hotel. He consoled himself with the fact that now he knew her name. Well, he would show patience too. She might not want to talk to him now but one day she would. He was sure of it.

Henry walked and walked and kept walking. The streets were quiet. The night air was punctured by a hollow laugh followed by the shutting of a door;

faint footsteps padded around a corner. The night sky turned purple, then black, before the moon rose. He watched it climb over the roofs, bright and clear, as he returned towards the beach. He kicked pebbles and stared through the angry barbed wire rolled against an untimely invasion whose immediacy had now passed. The tide had gone out leaving the decaying breakwaters rising out of the gloom like sentinels. The moon shone, its ghostly stare highlighting the barbed wire; silver thorns prevented any contemplation of a redemptive swim. He stood watching the moon-path over the ocean, watched its rippled surface; the direction fixed, straight, no deviation. The pebbles crunched and roared, shining pieces of rock beaten ever smaller as they jostled for prominence at his feet.

He bent down and chose a smooth, creamy-coloured one which he rolled briefly between his fingers before hurling it out to sea. Feverishly he picked up a handful and hurled one after another out into the oncoming moon-path. The outline wavered, broke into pieces and reformed unhesitatingly. Mercury droplets from a science class, separating and combining. The crash of the waves started talking to him: murmured, then more loudly, cried as they sucked the stones back under each other. The crying became sobbing, each indrawn breath releasing.

Henry turned from the water and walked back up towards the gun emplacement. As he rounded the corner the sobbing didn't fade; the whispering continued. A trick of the night? He hesitated, then walked forward. The shingle groaned under his feet as he moved toward the solid concrete wall, skimming his hand along its cold surface; the agonised whispers hushed. A sob was suppressed as he rounded the corner. Two huddled figures in bleached pink and lilac held up white faces, ghoulish in the dark with smudged lipstick and fiery eyes glittering.

His heart beat faster. The sound of the recent skirmish was in his ears; he could smell the smoke of the burning huts, hear the shrieks of the scared women and children subsiding into heart-wrenching sobbing, see the ripped garments.

"Go away; leave us alone."

As he surveyed the two pathetic figures, his breathing slowed. He raised his cap and attempted a concerned smile.

"Oh gosh, it's him. The one who's been following you everywhere."

"Leave us alone," Patience reiterated. 'We don't need you."

Grinding footsteps and muffled laughter sounded close as the girls, their faces flashing fear, scrambled to their feet, legs unsteady, slithering on the pebbles as they rushed past him.

Patience and Elsie fled up the beach towards the steep steps abutting the high sea wall. Henry stood his ground, cleared his throat loudly and menacingly, making enough noise on the stones for several men. He heard the girls' pursuers hesitate, saw their drunken shadows stumble in the opposite direction as he made his way after the two girls, his trot becoming a tiring walk as his feet slithered on the pebbles. He took the steps two at a time and sprinted along the promenade, catching up with the girls before they reached the pier. Hearing the pounding feet Patience spun around, her face a picture of blanched fear, a face shed of its masquerade, a marble statue streaked with stain.

"How many times do I have to tell you?" she gasped.

"Patience, don't, he's not an American. He's trying to help us."

"How d'you know? He could be in cahoots with them."

Henry opened his mouth to speak, disputed vehemently and assured them of his help. Patience pulled Elsie along, striding out in front of him, but Elsie was reluctant to relinquish the offered protection and looked back over her shoulder stubbornly, twisted out of Patience's grasp and waited for Henry to catch up with them.

"Don't leave us, please. Walk with us," Elsie said.

Patience's lips pursed and she shook her head but Elsie wanted to talk. Henry bristled with indignation as piece by piece the event was jigsawed together. The story gradually became clear through her tears. For every rip in her pink coat there was a story. Under the streetlamp he could see such youth and innocence in their faces.

"Just how old are you two?"

"Eighteen."

"Sixteen." They spoke in unison.

He looked from Elsie to Patience.

"Well, she's nearly seventeen and I'll be eighteen next year," Patience replied indignantly.

But her cape of confidence had slipped.

Chapter 3

August 2000
Bagni di Lucca, Tuscany

The road widened as he drove into the village. It was cooler here; dark shadows of the mountains gave welcome relief to heat-weary travellers. Henry saw a bunch of them, uniformly backpacked, with dirty trainers and greasy hair. They were hushed, creating only a dull buzz like somnolent flies, hunched in a group on the platform and occasionally glancing up the line; no train emerged from the tunnel.

Henry patted his hair, carefully combed over the bald patch. He glanced at his watch. He sat in the car methodically cleaning under his fingernails with the metal nail file attached to his key ring. Five minutes. Henry sat up straight, pushing his neck and back against the cushion. He pulled his shoulders down, closed his eyes and began rhythmically to tilt his head from side to side. He leant his head gently on the headrest.

April 1947
Rhyl, North Wales

"Keep down," he whispers to his men. "Don't move until I give the signal." Henry's voice is as taut as the belt around his waist; the butt of the gun digs into his chest. He tries to

21

swallow down the pounding in his throat.

"Captain Parker, there's a phone call for you." Mrs Richards rapped loudly on Henry's door. Henry shot forward in his chair, heart hammering in his chest.

"Captain Parker, are you in there? Telephone call for you."

Henry blinked. The machine-gun fire had stopped but someone was shouting.

"Captain Parker, Captain Parker, are you all right?"

"Yes, Mrs Richards... I'm fine... I must have just dozed off."

"Well, hurry along; a young lady is wanting to speak to you."

Henry cleared his throat, his heart still beating wildly in time to her heels clattering on the stair runners as he followed his landlady down into the hall where the telephone lay abandoned off the cradle.

"Hello. This is Captain Parker."

"Patience Tarmaster here. My mother said I should ring you to say thank you for walking us home last night."

"Oh. Miss Tarmaster. Don't... don't mention it. Glad to be of assistance." He relished the unfamiliar name, rolling it around his tongue, enjoying the experience of talking to her.

Silence. Then some whispering and rustling around the phone.

"Actually, Mummy has invited you round for tea. This afternoon."

"I would..."

"Oh, I know. It's such short notice, I told her you'd

be busy."

"No, I'm not, actually. I'd love to come."

Another cupped silence, as she placed her hand over the mouthpiece. More rustling and whispering.

"Mummy says you're to come at four o'clock. Everest is our house name, on Abercrombie Street, about halfway down on the left, by the horse chestnut tree."

"Thank you. I'll see you around four then. I'm looking forward…"

The phone clicked in his ear.

Henry hummed tunelessly as he combed his hair for the third time. He sat down on the bed but jumped up again and took out his shoe brush from his valet kit. The black shoes mirrored his smile. He checked his watch. Three o'clock. It wouldn't do to be late. It was at least a twenty-minute walk. He had better leave soon.

He whistled as he bounded down the stairs two at a time, stopping to straighten his tie once more in front of the hall mirror.

"If you're going out, Captain Parker, remember supper will be on the table at six o'clock sharp."

"Bye, Mrs Richards. I will be back in time. When have you ever known me to be late?" He allowed himself to chuckle.

Henry hastened his steps as he turned the corner into Abercrombie Street. He checked the house names and spotted the large horse chestnut, its tips drooping with white candles in full bloom. He looked at his watch and walked slowly past the gate and down to the end of the street. Children played in the little park across the road, running along the grey snaking paths edged with billowing daffodil-filled flowerbeds. He stopped to watch a boy of around six or seven who picked up a stick and ran behind a tree, peered out and aimed at a small girl in a pink dress coat. Henry froze as the boy shouted:

"Stop, or I'll shoot!"

Henry pulled out his handkerchief, wiped his top lip, pulled at his collar and kept his gaze on the girl. The boy ran up to her with his stick outstretched.

"You're supposed to die. I just shot you," he whined.

"Go away; I don't want to play anymore. Why do I always have to die?"

Henry hurried away, his shoes tapping out a jagged rhythm.

He paused before he reached the gate. He drew several deep breaths to calm himself, straightened his jacket and pushed open the wrought iron gate, which complained at his entry and set off a dog barking angrily from behind the neighbour's wall. How strange: the doorknocker was in the image of Ganesh, the elephant god. He had no time to ponder; before he could even check his watch, a tall Indian gentleman opened the door. Dressed in a pale suit and shiny chestnut brogues, he smiled at Henry.

"I'm sorry," said Henry; "I must have got the wrong house."

The man looked at Henry over his horn-rimmed spectacles.

"No, no, I don't think so. You must be Captain Parker. We are expecting you. Come in. Come in. Come and meet my wife."

Henry's whirling thoughts must have shown on

his face. The older man's brows lifted, and he looked enquiringly over his glasses.

Henry drew his manners smartly from behind his back together with his hand.

"Good afternoon, sir. Yes, Henry Parker. Pleased to meet you."

"Frank Tarmaster, Henry. Patience's father. Come this way. We're having tea in the conservatory."

Henry followed Frank Tarmaster's tall, slim figure down the hallway. He grinned. This explained so much: Patience's skin, and the exotic air she exuded. Desire washed over him, cleansing all thoughts but those of floundering in utter bliss, in her unblemished softness, unsullied by others, guided by his sense of rightness with the world. His covert glances assessed the kilims on the shiny floorboards. Golden balls surrounded a large round mirror suspended on a chain which reflected his surprised face as he gazed at the Indian silver filigree bowls on the sideboard. Mr Tarmaster was talking. Henry assented but had not heard a word he had been saying.

Mr Tarmaster opened French doors into a light-filled room. The afternoon sun was warming the glass of the conservatory, shedding green light through the imposing potted palms which threw shadowed fringes onto two seated figures. Patience and her mother sat facing each other on white rattan chairs.

"This is Henry Parker, my dear."

Henry barely glanced at the diminutive figure of her mother but smiled at Patience who seemed to be having trouble with a ring as she frowned and concentrated on her fingers, turning and turning the silver band with her other hand.

Mrs Tarmaster's smooth, plain face turned to him in greeting. She lifted a pale, limp hand to his.

"I'm so glad you could come, Captain. At such short notice, too."

He tore his gaze away.

"Pleased to meet you, Mrs Tarmaster."

"Well, we certainly wanted to meet you and thank you for saving our daughter and her silly little friend from those ghastly American soldiers. I'm sure it was all Elsie's fault."

"Mother... I've told you... it wasn't Elsie."

"Well. I don't know. You always seem to get into trouble when you are with her."

"Now, Maree, Captain Parker doesn't want to hear all this. We are just so glad you were there on the beach. Who knows what those GIs would have done? They seem to run a little wild here in town, you know. They think all the girls will fall for their charms."

"Oh, Father, they're not all bad, you know."

"Patience! How can you say that after last night? You need to be a little more careful, my girl."

Mrs Tarmaster turned a vague smile towards Henry.

"Captain Parker, may I call you Henry? Do you live near here? Are you posted nearby?"

"My dear. One question at a time. Poor Captain Parker."

Patience sighed and twisted a lock of hair.

"That's all right. Actually, I'm from Chorlton-cum-Hardy, in Manchester. My family moved from there to Bath some time ago."

"Really?" Mrs Tarmaster looked interested. "We came from Sale. We moved here because of the bombing. We used to come here for the holidays, so we knew the place quite well. I miss Manchester, though; I grew up there."

Henry was curious; did that mean Mr Tarmaster had grown up in Manchester too?

"My father was in the Royal Artillery and I followed him when I joined up," Henry said. "Actually," he ventured, "I'm stationed in India now, in Peshawar; I'm just here on leave."

Mr Tarmaster beamed. "What a coincidence! I grew up there and came over here to study." He laughed. "I met Maree and when I finished my degree we went back for a few years. In fact, both Patience and Max were born there." His face clouded. "The rest of my family are not so lucky to have another country to escape to."

Patience looked down at her lap, her attention drawn to a snagged thread on her houndstooth skirt. Henry looked at her bright green socks and smiled as he thought of emerald saris laid out to dry on riverbanks. Jewels in a dusty brown landscape.

He jumped as a door slammed fiercely, rattling the small panes in the French doors. Footsteps were heard on the stairs. Frank Tarmaster raised his eyebrows and getting up, shouted into the hallway.

"Max! I want to introduce you to Patience's saviour, Captain Parker. You're just in time for tea. Mrs Giles is bringing it any minute now." A muffled reply seemed to please Mr Tarmaster. "My son, Max. He'll join us in a few minutes."

Mrs Giles, with tightly curled grey hair and blue-flowered pinny, appeared on cue, rattling cups. She poured the tea without a glance at any of them. She straightened up with exaggerated slowness and shuffled out before Mrs Tarmaster thanked her.

"It's so difficult to get good help these days," she said.

Henry thought about smiling but catching Mr Tarmaster's nod he attempted a concerned look.

Max, it seemed, had just come back from work and as he shook hands with Henry his grasp was a tad tired, a tad weary. His eyes, however, were curious but welcoming. Tall and lean like his sister, he shared her olive colouring. Patience smiled warmly up at her brother who returned a complicit glance as he reached up to loosen his tie.

"Hello, Captain Parker. Or can I call you Henry? I'm pleased to meet you. How long are you here for?"

"Just a few weeks more, I think. I'm presuming they'll ship me back to Peshawar at the end of the month."

"Super. Not the shipping back I mean! Perhaps you can come with us to the dance at the holiday camp week after next. Do say yes; it's a really good place to meet girls." He stopped abruptly and laughed at Patience's expression.

"Aw, come on, sis, you know you like going. You and your friends are always talking about them. What officers you're going to meet. What you're going to wear."

"Well, now that you've met one, Patience dear, I'm sure he'll be happy to escort you and see you don't get into any more trouble," his father added.

Patience jiggled her foot furiously: a green lorikeet flapping its wings. Before she could protest there was another loud rap on the front door. Henry started. Patience jumped up.

"That'll be Elsie and her mother. I'll go and let them in."

Patience flew down the hallway and Henry could hear her talking to the new arrivals.

"So, Henry, you're about to meet the other grateful party, Mrs Rice. She does struggle to keep that girl in check."

Mr Tarmaster and Henry stood as Patience returned, pulling her petite friend along by the elbow. Elsie turned to look behind her, smiling at Max who was grinning widely as Patience sat down with Elsie away from her mother's gaze. Introductions completed, Mrs Rice sat down opposite Mrs Tarmaster. Henry hovered. He felt like a suitor in a Jane Austen novel his nanny had read to him when she had tired of Biggles and Billy Bunter. Possibly the hapless Mr Collins. He had always felt sorry for him; he wasn't exactly sure why.

Mrs Rice was talking loudly now.

"Captain Parker. Tell me what really happened last night." She turned back to Mrs Tarmaster. "Elsie's jacket was ruined, you know, torn on all that barbed wire still left on the beach." And without waiting for a comment, she addressed herself again to Henry. "Elsie said you chased off those scoundrels who had these poor young girls in their clutches. Fancy those soldiers picking on Patience and Elsie innocently walking home after visiting the amusement arcade! If your father were home, my girl… Of course, if it were me, I wouldn't have let them go off at that time" – she smiled sweetly at Mrs Tarmaster – "that's why you must be strict, you know; all those men roaming around from the camp." She paused and looked directly at Henry. "Well, at least you seem different, young man."

"I… but…" Henry caught Elsie's pleading glance and hesitated before telling Mrs Rice how glad he had been to help. Or he nearly managed to say that before Mrs Rice was holding forth once more on dastardly male doings and badly brought-up young females.

"Tea, Mrs Rice?" ventured Mr Tarmaster as he attempted to stop the flow. Unsuccessful, he went off in search of more biscuits.

Elsie and Patience, deep in conversation, did not rescue Henry from Mrs Rice's attention. What were they talking about? Could Patience be talking about him? Henry listened to how hard it was for Mrs Rice with Mr Rice away training, how nobody understood how difficult it was to bring up a daughter these days. Max, offering around biscuits, pulled a face at Henry. Why was this horrid woman insisting on talking at him? Henry glanced at Patience, but he felt like a naughty schoolboy and brought his attention back to what Mrs Rice was saying. Damn, it was a question. Pity it wasn't about how the light from the window changed the colour of Patience's hair or how she jiggled her foot every time she talked or how she flicked a stray curl from her forehead or tucked another behind her ear in a characteristic gesture.

"Elsie, have you heard anything I've been saying? I was asking Henry if he'd come to dinner next Saturday."

Seeing the stricken looks on both of Elsie's and

Max's faces, Patience piped up.

"This Saturday? Max, isn't that when we've all arranged to go to the pictures at the holiday camp?"

"Pictures? Oh, yes, that's right. Sorry, Mrs Rice. Henry and Elsie are coming with us."

Henry looked at Patience in surprise. She had studiously avoided talking to him and now she was including him in arrangements. Perhaps she did like him after all.

Deflated, Mrs Rice stopped talking and devoured her biscuit and tea with the same gusto she had put into her monologue. Mrs Tarmaster twisted her handkerchief, looking up as her husband came back into the room with yet another plate of biscuits.

"I have asked Mrs Giles to put out more than one biscuit each… but you know what a Lancashire upbringing does to you." His wife managed a wan smile.

Chapter 4

April 1947
Rhyl, North Wales

As Henry walked back to the boarding house, his mind was a jumble of thoughts tumbling around needing to be shaken out, folded and put away into appropriate drawers.

Patience had invited him out on Saturday night. Patience had included him in her plans. Patience, who had hardly said a word to him all afternoon, had, without prompting, asked him out. When would be a good time to phone her? Should he call tomorrow? Or should he wait? Should he call on the pretext of thanking Mrs Tarmaster for tea? What was he thinking? Of course he should do that. Yes, that would be best. He should do that anyway. How many times had the teachers drummed into him, "Manners maketh the man"? "Spare the rod, spare the child." How many times had he written that on a page, letters reaching out to each other in their agony, grasping hands, trying to offer consolation, balm to the stinging slices behind his knees? Bless me, Father, for I have sinned.

Thank you, God, for looking after me. Thank you, Patience. Thank you, Mrs Tarmaster. Thank you, Frank Tarmaster. Oh, and thank you, Mrs Giles, for bringing in the tea. Thank you, Nanny, for reading to me at night. Thank you, Mother, for teaching me to behave. He walked past a large oak tree at the corner of the park which reeked of the acrid smell of dog piss like the stinking wetness of his shorts when he was dragged before Father Gerolomi to confess his sins.

Running up the dark hallway he hears the brittle laughter of his mother, the Marmite tones of Father Gerolomi behind the sitting room door. Standing outside the closed door he watches his chest move in and out, the pattern on his jumper expanding and contracting. As his breathing becomes more regular, he realises the rattling of china cups has ceased. Instead, he hears breathing, sighs and the rustling of fabric.

Henry wipes the toe of one of his muddy shoes behind his sock. He wipes his hands down the sides of his jacket and picks off a stray piece of goosegrass attached to his shorts. He is late for tea. Mother usually wants him to come in and say hello to Father Gerolomi first. She will hold him tight, cover his small face with kisses and caress him, her cold hands running up and down his bare legs. Father Gerolomi's eyes will follow her hands' trail up and down her son's body as the boy squirms knowing how this excessive loving will be followed by a rapid ushering off to the nursery and an admonition to tell Nanny to read to him. The door is shut tight. Does this mean he should knock and loudly announce his lateness, or will it be better to reach up, turn the handle slowly, holding it tight, and push the door open by degrees? Henry wavers; he feels he will be in trouble either way. Valour overcomes discretion and he stands on tiptoe to turn the handle. The brass handle is so shiny that he sees it wink back at him as his hand grasps it. In the wedge of revealed room, he sees his mother being smothered by Father Gerolomi. Startled, he notices the cassock is up around the Father's waist, his hairy buttocks muscling in and out. Henry watches, fascinated, as his mother moans. She's still alive. He decides he should run upstairs. He doesn't want to be blamed for killing her. He races upstairs as a lump of coal falls with a clatter out of the grate onto the tiled fireplace.

"Henry. Is that you?" Not dead yet. She has enough puff to shout. Maybe he is wrong. His mother says he usually is.

Chapter 5

April 1947
Rhyl, North Wales,

Saturday was a long day. Henry busied himself; he wrote to his mother; he went to the post office and sent the letter, although he would have preferred to send it on Monday when he might have been able to run into Patience, but he had to let his mother know when he was coming to visit; he walked along the promenade trying to quieten himself. He walked to the station and booked a ticket to go down to Bath on Wednesday. Earlier in the week, his father had told him he could not put off coming home any longer; he was to write to his mother, who was having the vapours, and tell her when he was arriving.

"There's a telegram come for you, Captain," Mrs Richards said from the lounge as he opened the front door. She bustled out the better to see his face as he opened it.

Henry murmured his thanks but to Mrs Richards' disappointment, he put it in his breast pocket. She followed him with her eyes, head tilted, as he made his way up the stairs, but Henry did not look behind him or give her any satisfaction.

As he entered his room, he sighed and sat down on the bed. He knew what the telegram would say. It would be from his father, again stating that he had to come home right now as his mother had taken a turn for the worse. A tactic she had used before to force him to visit when he showed no inclination of so doing. He might have to go before Wednesday, which meant he would have to tell Patience tonight that he was leaving; not that she would probably care.

He gave his notice to Mrs Richards who told him how sorry she was to lose him and that she had hoped that he was going to spend all his leave at her boarding house. Henry told her that his mother was ill and he had to return home. He spent the rest of the morning packing, folding and refolding clothes into his trunk.

The bell for lunch rang loudly, angrily. It must have been the second time Mrs Richards had rung it. Henry's stomach was churning. He was not sure that he could eat anything.

"Captain Parker? Are you coming down for lunch?" Mrs Richards' querulous voice warbled up the stairs. Henry stood up slowly, opened the door and called down.

"I'm sorry, Mrs Richards. I'll be down in a minute. I must've fallen asleep." He made his way slowly down into the dining room. He hated being the last to be seated. The frozen smile on Mrs Richards' face had probably cooled the soup. He was glad of the soup, though: potato and onion. A soup that even Mrs Richards could not ruin. The Davies sisters, identically dressed but in hand-knitted cardigans of a different colour, one green, one blue, each ventured a nervous smile towards Henry before finishing off their soup. Their spoons clattered against the bowls in the silence. Miss Hughes of the trailing scarves asked Henry nervously when he was leaving. Henry was glad to break the quiet, to override the soft slurps of soup.

"I am leaving on Wednesday, Miss Hughes. My mother is unwell and I really must go home."

General commiseratory murmurs erupted and there was much shaking of grey locks as the lodgers envisaged similar scenarios for themselves and wondered who would come to visit them in their hour of need.

Henry excused himself from the table and went back upstairs. He felt nervous and although he had spoken to Patience during the week to confirm the arrangements for tonight, he was uneasy. He spent several minutes inspecting his clothing for lint, several minutes checking between his teeth, several minutes trying out another jumper. He felt anxious and the suspense in the room increased until he had to get out and walk along the promenade, aware that he was much too early for the arranged rendezvous. The crashing grey waves boomed in his ears and followed the thudding of his heart. Patience's laughing smile emerged from the sea, her head covered with an iridescent sari. No. He shook his head. That's wrong. Patience didn't wear saris. Patience was here in Wales. Another image arose from the waves: blood streaming down a face, sunset streaks across the water. He turned abruptly and made his way to the holiday camp. The churning in his stomach subsided as he walked along the pavement, his shoes clicking.

This was not ordinary; he had a feeling about this girl, he wasn't sure what. Destiny had put her in his way but how it would play out he did not know. He had no experience of this feeling, but he had never felt so convinced of anything before.

As he turned onto Sea Road, he raised his eyes and noted streams of young people making their way towards the gates of the holiday camp where the film was to be shown. It was a popular event. As arranged, he stood just outside the booth where the holiday camp guard was checking tickets on a battered clipboard. Henry was amused to see that he wore a cap, a military-style cap, although he was the furthest from a military man, his dusty jacket unbuttoned at the top button, the frayed ends of his shirt protruding. It had been a hard war and it was perhaps harder now with continued rationing for the good people of North Wales, he mused. He ground out his cigarette with his heel and pulled down his jacket hem as he saw a pink coat coming around the corner.

Elsie was laughing up at Patience whose dark hair swung in front of her cheek, only a slash of bright lipstick visible. He watched as they came closer; Patience raised her hand in greeting. He smoothed down his hair with his cupped hand and patted his neck at the collar – almost as if he were himself a good dog; an affectionate gesture, maybe the precursor to the pinch of his mother's fingers pushing him out of the drawing-room, calling out for Nanny to take him up to the playroom for his supper.

He waved back and smiled a shy smile. Patience stopped talking and said by way of greeting that Max had phoned the house to say that he would be late and would meet them there. After enquiring how they both were (he did not dare to refer to the incident on the beach), the conversation lagged. Patience almost jiggled from foot to foot as she glanced up the road. Elsie smiled at Henry.

"There he is," Patience said, as a ruffled Max turned the corner from Wood Street and made his way towards them. It was clear he had been running.

"I'm so sorry, Elsie," he said, addressing himself only to her. He clasped her hand and continued, "You know I wouldn't have been late if I could've helped it. The bank, you know, they want their pound of flesh."

"Oh, come on, stop making googly eyes!" Patience grabbed his other arm. "We don't want to miss the shorts, do we?"

They turned, dragging him off, but Max called back to Henry.

"Good to see you, Henry. Come on. Follow us in. Patience, have you got the tickets?"

Patience pulled four tickets out of her velvet-topped coat pocket and presented them to the camp guard.

"Evening, Miss. Hope you enjoy the film. S'posed to be a funny'n."

As they waited to go inside Henry looked at the poster. Hmm. Blithe Spirit. Well, is that how he seemed? Or would the epithet suit Max? He seemed more earnest than blithe. It was obvious to Henry that Elsie was more to him than just his sister's friend.

Patience was talking to a blonde girl waiting further up the queue. Henry thought she looked familiar and wondered if he might have seen her in the bank where Patience worked. Perhaps she was another teller.

"Beryl says this is supposed to be a really good comedy. It's based on a Noel Coward play, you know. I just love his writing, don't you?" Patience asked Henry.

Henry was not sure if he had read any of Coward's

work and said so, at which Patience raised an eyebrow and said, "Well, at least you must have heard of Constance Cummings; anyway, she plays the new bride."

Henry wondered if he had heard of Constance Cummings. He started to say that he wasn't that up on film stars, having been far from thinking about popular culture during the war in India; but Patience cut across him and said to Max, "Let's sit in the middle at the back. We'll have the best view there."

Elsie giggled, and looking at Henry's horrified face she started to blush. An unbecoming pink, thought Henry; it clashed with her – now neatly-mended – coat. Patience laughed.

"Oh, you. That's not what I meant at all. I don't want to sit with all the lovebirds canoodling and cooing. I don't suppose you do either, do you, Henry?"

It was Henry's turn to feel the prickle of embarrassment as a red flush spread from his collarbones, turning his neck scarlet blotched with white. Patience laughed. "I bet you're glad it's getting dark."

"Don't be so cruel, Patience," said Max. "Leave the poor chap alone. I don't think he's used to being teased, are you, Henry?"

Henry blustered and felt the heat increase and rise to his cheeks. He was spared by the queue moving forward; and Patience's interest in finding the best seats took away her attention from his discomfort.

"Well, I'm not sure it was such a good film," said Patience as they walked out of the improvised theatre;

"it felt old-fashioned to me. You know, a bit Victorian for my liking…"

"Oh, not at all," said Max. "I just loved how it showed up social politics…"

"Oh Max," said Elsie, "that's all you think about, isn't it? Politics, politics, politics! Nothing about everyday things, you know, important things…"

"What, like make-up and where you can get the best dress?" Max scoffed.

Another blush threatened and even though Elsie felt that Patience's arm around her was meant to give her courage, she stiffened, eyes glistening.

"That was a bit rough, Max, old man," ventured Henry.

"I'm sorry, love," said Max. "I had a busy day and you know how I get."

Ah ha, thought Henry. I was right. These two do have something going on. Something, he felt, that neither of their parents knew about or would approve of. Young love. How old was she? He struggled to remember. Seventeen, he thought, or nearly so.

"Come along." Patience tucked her arm under his and said to Max and Elsie, "We're going for a drink; are you coming? Kiss and make up, all right?"

Max's long frame relaxed, and he smiled a crooked smile at Elsie, a dimple appearing to the left of his lips. Henry flashed a look at Patience; he was sure she had a similar dimple, but he just couldn't remember.

The bar room in the holiday camp was crowded. The floor felt sticky and the air was already thick with cigarette smoke. Various officers lounged against the chipped edge of the bar, some of whom Henry recognised, but being out of uniform he had no need to salute, receive salutations or even acknowledge them. He enjoyed that feeling.

"I'll get the first round," Max said. "What would you like?"

Patience and Elsie were not out to impress, he thought; they asked for half a shandy each and went to sit in the snug.

"Well, Henry," Max said as they waited to be served, "am I right in thinking that you've taken quite a fancy to my sister?"

"I… I think she is very b-b-beautiful," Henry stammered.

"Yes, she's quite a looker, isn't she? A bit of a terror, really. I could tell you some stories! Two pints, please, and two half shandies."

A terror? What did Max mean? Henry clasped two of the glasses and strode after Max to the corner where Patience and Elsie were deep in conversation.

"Well, excuse us," said Max, "here's your drinks and do let us in on the juicy titbits you two were discussing."

"It was nothing," said Patience; and her eyes cut across to Elsie almost imperceptibly.

But Henry noticed. He felt he would notice any expression, any fleeting thought or emotion which flickered across her face. Elsie tossed her head and curled a strand around her middle finger. Patience smacked it out of her hand.

"Stop being coy," Patience snapped; and for the second time within ten minutes Elsie's emotions threatened to spill.

"Patience, stop it," said Max, as he held out his hand to Elsie and gave hers a gentle squeeze. "She can be so beastly sometimes; don't you mind her."

Henry watched, curious. He felt as though he was still watching the film; watching Elvira, the mischievous ghost wife. No, this couldn't be right. Patience is an angel. Patience shook her head.

"You know I'm only teasing, Elsie. I'm sorry. Come on, cheer up, let's not spoil a good evening."

Her mercurial change was infectious and the tension lessened as they all began to talk at once and ended up laughing. Even Henry was laughing, although he did not know why.

He saw dark eyes, laughing up at him. He saw dark eyes glinting above a mustard-coloured sari. He smelt jasmine and leaned over, closer, to inhale its intoxifying scent.

"Henry! I don't know you that well," Patience chided, and he sat back in his seat, dazed.

Chapter 6

1947
Bath

Patience hugged herself with delight. It would be wonderful for Elsie and Max to spend some time away from their respective watchful parents.

Henry was not sure how his mother would react to hosting three of his friends for a weekend but if that were the price she paid for having him visit, she would probably do her best to be civil and would rise out of her funk to be the gracious hostess. She would shake off the indeterminate headaches and weaknesses to arrange a sparkling dinner party. Henry had come up with the idea as they all sat chatting together after the pictures. He had told them he was going to Bath to his parents' and it seemed a great way to get to know Patience better whilst pretending that it was for the benefit of Elsie and Max.

The golden stone of Bath greeted Henry as he got off the train and made his way up Gay Street to the Circus. It was colder today; the swirl of a breeze with an eastern chill nipped at his ears. Summer was not yet here.

He paused as the road opened out and he wondered at the dignity of the buildings, how they had been battered and abused by war but with rubble mostly cleared away still managed to look grand. The huge bomb disposal crater loomed large in the centre of the Crescent, the branches of the trees casting skeletal patterns.

His mother greeted him as he entered the drawing-room. She sat on the sofa, a blanket around her knees. A languid hand was stretched up for him to kiss and she pulled him to her, proffered her powdered cheek and smiled.

"I'm feeling so much better now you're here, Henry. You're very naughty not to have come down to see me before." She patted the sofa beside her. "Come and tell me all about India. I'm so glad you're here now. The news of all the dreadful killings has reached us even here in Bath. I hope they'll sort it out soon! I hope you didn't have to see any of that."

Henry's eyes glazed. The dust from the sofa tickled his nostrils and he began to sneeze.

As he sneezes he can see the dust whirling around the marketplace. Running footsteps retreat and, horrified, he stares at the bodies sprawled at his feet as the gunshots fade.

The footsteps became his father's as he entered the room and shook his son's hand. "Good to see you, old boy."

"I hope he hasn't brought me a cold," his mother said petulantly. "I am still feeling so frail. That would be the end of me, I'm sure."

Henry stopped mid-sneeze and remembered that he had brought her some flowers; they were out on the hall table and would surely make her feel better.

"So, what are your plans, dear boy? Are they going to call you back?"

His mother and father knew little of the events

he had endured. Indeed, he had told everyone he was on leave, not that he was recovering from witnessed atrocities. He was not going to tell them. They would not understand. He did not need platitudes and sympathy which would be brushed over in a minute as the perceived important issues of continued rationing or the difficulties of maintaining good servants rose to the fore in his mother's consciousness.

"Why are you both here in Bath? Surely it's more comfortable in the country?" he asked them.

"Well, you know what your father's like. He needs to be near the surgery."

"Me?" his father replied indignantly.

It was an old argument and Henry did not want to fall into the whirlpool of recriminations and innuendo and so took himself off to his room, claiming tiredness after his journey.

"He looks exhausted." His father looked at his mother. "I'm sure even you can see a hollowness in his eyes; perhaps best not to talk about India, eh?"

The few days he spent in Bath before Patience, Max and Elsie arrived were not restful. He wandered around the town. Such pointless destruction. Tit for tat, he recalled. Lubeck and its fine wooden buildings destroyed first and then Bath had its blitz the following month. Hard to see the sense in any of it. Blocks of stone, rubble from the Francis Hotel at the south side of Queen Square, still littered the gardens. He recalled the letter he had received from his mother whilst he was sipping a gin and tonic on a veranda in Burma before he was posted to Peshawar.

49

Dear Henry,

You are so lucky not to be here. We're fortunate that we were at Redlands when the bombs fell on Bath. Yes, on Bath, can you believe it? We didn't think that the Luftwaffe would bother with Bath when they had Bristol in their sights every night but it seems as though they didn't take lightly our brave lads' bombing of Lubeck last month. An eye for an eye as the good book says. It never seems to have the same veracity when you're on the receiving end, though.

Your father, luckily, was here with me as there was a hit on the Circus and can you believe, the Crescent. Can't see that we had anything the Huns would want but luckily the houses weren't destroyed completely like poor St. Andrew's Church; it's just a shell of itself. They're talking of pulling it down it's so dangerous. Francis Hotel has gone and the assembly rooms which, as you know, we contributed to for the restoration, also completely gone. I wonder how long it will be before our beautiful Bath returns to normality? How long is this beastly war going to go on for?

But I shouldn't be pessimistic. You're facing much worse where you are. I worry every day that a telegram might come... Oh, there I go again thinking about bad things.

The gardens are wonderful; the roses have never looked so beautiful after such a long, cold winter. The Madame Alfred Carriere that I planted on the wall by the conservatory is just splendid. It has completely covered it in just one season. Take that, Herr Hitler!

Father Gerolami sends his best wishes and says he is praying for you. I do hope you are remembering to say yours.
Write soon,
Yours affectionately,
Mother

As he walked, he wondered whether he should visit an old school friend who lived nearby, further along Charlotte Street; but then he remembered that he too was away in India with the Glosters.

Images rose again before his eyes: jewel colours, dust and dirt, screams and shouts becoming louder and louder as he drew to a halt, confused, turning this way and that looking for the source. His leaping pulse threatened to burst his collar and he wiped the sweat from his forehead with his sleeve. He sat on a bench, the underneath of which was strewn with scrunched up small red and white paper bags, their sweet contents long gone; he dropped his head in his hands and drew some deep breaths as the doctor had advised.

Children; just children, playing in the park. Rest and recuperate; you will soon be fine, the doctor had said. Fine for what, he thought? Fine to return to that hell hole of partition, to the sweeping violence and nonsensical loss of culture? Perhaps, yes, he should return to Peshawar and help. Help others. No, he needed to stay here, to see Patience. He would not go back.

A muddle of voices rose from the hall: his mother's

dulcet tones with the familiar veneer of forced politeness she used when greeting new acquaintances, Max's baritone, Elsie's piping greeting; and above all, the melodic, mannered Patience.

"I'm so delighted to meet you. Thank you so much for having us. Henry has told us so much about you."

Henry raced down the stairs two at a time and jumped onto the Afghan rug, nearly tripping in his eagerness. His mother watched him with an arched brow.

"Well, that's the most energy you've expended since coming home. I'm so glad to see you with a smile."

Henry smoothed back his hair with that characteristic patting gesture and grinned at them all. Then he was embarrassed. Behaving like a schoolboy. It wouldn't do at all. He cleared his throat.

"Come, I'll show you to your rooms. I'm afraid they're on the second floor but Mother insists that if guests wish to stay they'll be happy to make the extra climb!"

It was a tonic, those few days. Elsie and Max in their own little world chatted about plans, life and love. Henry in his customary shyness around Patience listened intently to her prattle. He took note of complementary colours as they ranged themselves against Patience, as they walked through the Botanic Gardens wrapped up warmly in scarves and hats against the unseasonal chill. Rather early for the full burgeoning of summer colour; nevertheless, a few acers glowed through branches of the canopied oaks. A winding path took them to the Temple of Minerva.

"Hurry up, you two, stop dawdling. Look at this,

hidden away in the trees. Isn't it beautiful?"

The four stood, gazing up at Aquae Sulis inscribed above the perfectly arched doorways.

"How did they build something so beautiful so long ago and in such a wonderful spot?" Elsie said finally.

"This isn't old!" Henry said. "They built it for the 1924 British Empire Exhibition at Wembley, to advertise Bath and its antiquities. I'll take you to the Baths tomorrow. Sadly, the assembly rooms were utterly destroyed and many of the other Roman buildings damaged. You'll see. We didn't get spared from a blitz as you did in North Wales."

"Well, how did it get to be here then if it was in London?" Elsie asked.

Max looked at her fondly as Henry explained how they had labelled every stone and brought them back here to the gardens and reconstructed the temple for all to enjoy.

"Oh," she said, feeling rather small and foolish. Max put his arm around her and squeezed.

"Never mind, my love. We all learn things by asking."

That weekend Henry imprinted Patience onto his memory, learnt her by heart and photographed her in his mind as she laughed when they swept up the Lansdown Road towards the racecourse. It was windy and she kept tucking her hair behind her ear, a long curl escaping over and over.

Patience yelled to Max and Elsie sitting crunched in the back of his father's car: "You'll have to get Henry to teach you yoga if the journey's too long!"

Henry heard her, even though her words were snatched out of her mouth and sent over the hedge, darting around the boys playing rugby on the playing fields. It was a jewelled moment for him, a freeze frame of exquisite joy. His heart was banging on his ribs, a good tune, but he was frightened to smile, to appear ridiculous in her eyes. He focused on the road ahead.

"I hope you'll all come to church with us tomorrow," his mother offered. After such a wonderful evening meal, Patience smiled, and Max and Elsie could do little else but agree that they would love to; and they dutifully rose at the appointed time.

They knocked on Patience's door.

"Patience, come on. Henry and his mother are waiting for us to have breakfast so we can walk together to St Mary's."

Elsie opened the door to a tousled head of dark curls peeping above a flowered eiderdown.

"It's so warm in here. It's cold outside; I'm sure there's a frost on the window. I might just stay here; so cosy…" she drifted.

"Oh, Patience, Mrs Parker will be so upset. She particularly wanted us to see the new stained-glass windows."

No answer. Gentle rhythmic breathing.

"Patience is so tired, Mother. She would love to come but she's been working too hard lately and is just so fatigued."

A harrumph from his mother indicated that attending church was one of the prerequisites of a stay at her house, however exhausted one might be.

"Well, Father isn't coming."

"He never does, Henry. You know that."

Max and Elsie chattered on. They were all grateful for the extra coats which Mrs Parker had urged on them. Cuddled together, Elsie's tiny hand was clasped in Max's in the pocket of his overcoat.

The new stained glass was duly admired by all and while Henry and his mother went up for the sacrament, Max and Elsie cuddled closer on the mahogany pew and shivered both with cold and the delight of being able to spend so much time together. Elsie's mother had known she was going with Patience to Bath, which was cause enough for concern in her eyes; but of course, the name of Max had not been mentioned. Patience's mother knew they were all three going but in her naïve gentility did not see that there might be some impropriety.

Patience meandered down to the breakfast room to see Henry's father half-hidden behind the Times, spooning lukewarm scrambled eggs into himself.

"Good morning, Patience. You managed to escape purgatory this morning, did you? Won't endear you to Mrs Parker, you know."

Patience shrugged.

"Good morning, Doctor Parker. It was just so cold. I was so snuggly I just couldn't get up. I'm sorry, I didn't mean to be rude."

Once the church-goers returned, it was not long before Sunday lunch was served. No rationing in evidence here. Mrs Blake the housekeeper brought in a leg of lamb, sprigged with rosemary and garlic (Mrs Parker's Mediterranean influence, no doubt). It sat steaming on a grand serving dish surrounded by crisped potatoes, parsnips and swedes.

"I do hope you eat swedes. Needs must, you know. We would never have dreamt of eating them before the war. Animal food. But they're quite delicious the way Mrs Blake prepares them."

Patience, Max and Elsie all murmured assent but Mrs Parker had not addressed Patience. She studiously avoided making eye contact with her throughout the meal; and it was with relief that Patience packed her bag to leave that afternoon.

"Hurry up," she called out to Elsie and Max. "We'll miss the train. I can't wait to leave and Mrs Parker can't wait to see the back of me!"

"Your mother hates me!" she said to Henry as he stood on the platform waving goodbye.

"Of course she doesn't hate you! But... well, if you'd gone to church, I think she'd certainly have been happier. I've certainly enjoyed the weekend."

Through the carriage window Henry could see three heads and three waving hands. He walked alongside the train as it gathered speed.

"I'll let you know when I'm leaving here, if that's okay!" he shouted as he ran to keep up with it.

Henry stood by the breakfast room window whilst bone china cups tinkled on the table, his mother's signal to 'Stop dreaming and come and have breakfast'. She cleared her throat with an exaggerated cough to gain Henry's attention.

"She's certainly very striking, Henry, but she isn't a Catholic, and won't even attend a Sunday service," she said to his back.

Henry didn't answer.

A boy in a blue uniform on a bicycle came into the Circus and Henry could see him looking up at house numbers. With a sinking heart, Henry saw the boy throw down his bike and, grasping a piece of paper in his hand, take the steps to his parents' house two at a time. He was whistling: a tune Henry knew but could not place. It suddenly was very important that he knew, more important than the telegram, more important than India, more important than anything. He raced to the door and opened it.

"For you, sir," the young lad said.

"What were you whistling?"

"Whistling? Was I, sir? Sorry, I won't do it again."

"No, no; it's fine. I just want to know what it was. Do you know its name?"

"Don't rightly remember, sir. Could have been 'Heartaches' or even 'When You Were Sweet Sixteen'; yeah, that would be it, sir."

He touched his cap and grinned. Henry placed a penny in his outstretched hand. The boy frowned and looked down. Henry hastily added some more change, a threepence and some more pennies, until the boy smiled and took away his hand and placed the coins in his pocket. Jingling and whistling, he turned back down the steps.

Henry stared at the telegram. He did not wish to read the words. He placed it on the silver tray in the hall but then took it up again and started to go upstairs.

"Who was that, dear?'

"No one. Nothing important. I'm just going upstairs

for a while. I'll come down for coffee later."

But it was important. It was a notification to send him back. He knew it without opening it. All that remained to be known was when. His stomach clenched and unclenched, astringent bile flooded his mouth, and he raced to the bathroom.

Chapter 7

June 1947
Peshawar, India

Dear Patience,
    I am so sorry that I was not able to come
back to Wales before I left for Peshawar. My mother
kept me in Bath for more days than I wanted and
then I got the telegram to return to Peshawar. It all
seemed to happen so suddenly even though I was
expecting it any day.

I must tell you that the few days you stayed in
Bath with me were probably the happiest of my
life. It is a long time since I have enjoyed anything
so much. I certainly didn't enjoy the return
journey back here to Peshawar; the boat seemed
to take longer than usual. One event which might
amuse you happened on the train from Bombay.
As I think I told you there are always wallahs
trying to sell you something. One watch seller had
a case full of watches. He was demonstrating how
good they were by opening one up to show the
workings. I just laughed but Higgins parted with
some money and took off back to his carriage with
his prize. He just kept winding and winding the
stem but nothing made it work! It was obviously
a dud. He and some others set off up the train to
find the trickster and give him what for! I thought
I had better follow to make sure they didn't get

into any trouble. We found him plying his wares to some other unsuspecting fellow. Higgins grabbed his case and threw it and all the watches out of the train window. The wallah twisted out of Higgins' grasp and tried to follow his case out of the window but they held onto him. "We won't hurt him, sir."

They told me later they put him down about 100 miles up the track when the train slowed down for water. Can you believe the poor fellow had to walk all the way home from there with no watches? Well, I suppose he won't try that again!

I hope you don't mind me writing but I would like it most awfully if you could write back and tell me all your news to brighten my day in this mixed-up hell-hole. We will be leaving soon, I think, or so we've been told.

I probably shouldn't tell you, but you may have guessed what I feel about you and don't tell me I hardly know you because I feel as if I have always known you!

There, I've said it – you don't have to mention it if you don't want to, just don't tell me I'm out of order as I will live for the days your letters arrive!
Yours,
Henry

Chapter 8

June 1947

Dear Henry,
     Of course I will write to you. Anything to cheer up an officer!

I know I'm mean but not that mean. After all, you helped Elsie and me out of a real pickle.

I guess you knew all along that they were sweet on each other, didn't you? Max and Elsie, I mean. Max doesn't want Mother and Father to know and as for Elsie's mother, she would be really angry as she says Elsie is far too young to be stepping out with anybody. Although I don't think Max is just 'anybody', he's my darling brother! They've managed to get away with it so far, the parents didn't even twig about the visit to Bath, as we've all been friends for so long.

Mother had a group of lady friends around for tea yesterday, boring, and I had to be polite and help be a hostess. All they talked about was rationing and how badly we young ones all behaved. Didn't behave like that in our day, blah, blah, etc. etc!

Back to the 'morgue' tomorrow after a few days' holiday. I wish I could do something different, but Father still seems to think that it's a good job for a girl and being an accountant, of course, he thinks banking is wonderful! I don't!

Anyway, write when you can and keep your chin up. You'll be back in the old Blighty soon.

Patience

June 1947

My dear Patience,

It was so good to read your news and think of you at your boring job waiting for the clock to strike five. Time passes here slowly too. Some days are awful, there are still so many atrocities and we're forced to go out on patrol to see to burning buildings and civilian casualties. I often feel light-headed. The other day, Higgins asked if I was all right as he said I was just standing there staring at the flames of a shantytown just around the corner from the barracks. The situation really makes me angry and mostly I blame Jinnah for his pig-headedness in insisting on the split. What a mess. Do you hear much about it over there?

But enough of that. I want to hear all about you. Where you go, what you do and who you see. I don't know when I will be back, but I hope that you won't mind if I come to visit you.

Yours affectionately, (do you mind?)

Henry

p.s. I may be assigned to quartermaster duties soon which I think will suit me well!

Dear Henry,

I'm so glad you'll get a change of duties. It sounds as though you need it with those frightful headaches and now the light-headedness.

Life is the same here. Abergele is getting back to normal and there seem to be fewer and fewer officers around. Poor me! Fewer partners for the dances! I must say, though, that everyone I meet is really good fun, except those horrible Americans of course. I won't make that mistake again. Anyway, I hear they'll be long gone when you return.

I'm going to the pictures tonight to see The Seventh Veil. James Mason's starring – ooh, I do like him!

Elsie and her mother have gone to stay with her grandmother for a month up somewhere in Yorkshire, near Huddersfield, I think. I'll miss her – and so will Max! I wondered if Mrs Rice had caught wind of their little romance. I hope not, or we'll never see Elsie again...

I'm sorry you're still getting those headachy things or whatever they are. I'm sure they'll go once you're away from India. You know I don't remember too much about life there, but I do remember how intense the colours seemed, I loved my ayah's saris and always wanted to wrap myself in the bright silk, so soft. I'd take the edge, you know where the gold embroidery starts, and just rub it between my fingers and lay my cheek against it until I fell asleep! Funny what memories you have.

Well, take care of yourself, and look forward to hearing from you again soon,
Patience

Henry sat on the veranda, rocking gently, glad of the breeze the movement afforded him. He sipped his gin and tonic slowly, feeling the tartness and fizz scouring a path down his dry throat. He looked down Ali Mardan Khan's palace garden, the billet for the army cantonment, and watched as Sunita gathered the mangoes into the basket she had at her feet. She turned and smiled back at him.

"Well, I don't think Gandhi is going to manage this without some bloodshed," said Captain John Watts.

"I think Jinnah has been awfully pig-headed really. I just don't see how these two countries are going to work. Look at Sunita. She and her family have always lived here. Asking them to leave and relocate to a Hindu territory down south is asking for trouble."

"Well, as usual, we'll be the last to know when these things are going to happen. Mountbatten seems to be playing his cards close to his chest."

Henry sighed and wiped the condensation off the bottom of his glass, leaving a wet smudge on his khaki trousers.

"I've told Sunita and her parents to leave, to gather their things and go; but they won't believe that any of their friends would turn on them, and they like working here at the palace. Her father was born here. Did you know his father worked here too? This is their life. I don't think they've ever gone more than a few miles from Peshawar."

"Of course this would have nothing to do with Sunita not wanting to leave you, would it?" John laughed. "She is exquisitely beautiful. Her skin must be so soft…"

Henry interrupted him. "What are you implying exactly? Sunita is about to be married. I have nothing but respect for her."

John chortled into his glass, making Henry bristle and stand up quickly. "I suggest you don't talk about things you know nothing about. Stick to military strategy, John; at least you know something about that. I'm going to bathe and get ready for dinner now. I'll see you later."

John continued sitting there, his stocky legs firmly planted on the floor, cooling the sweating patches behind his knees and between his legs. He could still see Sunita, her emerald green sari bright against the dusty trees as she reached up for another mango, picking them for the green chutney the officers so enjoyed. The setting sun outlined her slim figure. She picked up the basket and started walking up the path, her bangles tinkling, her kohl-ringed eyes smudged dark in the dying light. As she caught him staring at her she picked up the tail of her sari and shyly wrapped it around her face, her coal dark eyes contrasting with the brilliance of the silk.

"Good evening, Miss Mehra. What delights are you going to cook for us tonight?"

"Good evening, sahib." The rest of her reply was muffled under the sari and he contented himself with continuing to watch as she gracefully trod up the stairs to the kitchen. He stood and stretched, his shirt falling off his back, the sweat cooling.

At dinner, the conversation picked up where it had left off. The three officers at the table had their own opinions.

"I really can't see what the fuss is about. Obviously, it'll work. You just have to get them back to where they belong. Such a mess having all these religions in one place," offered Corporal Hamilton as he took yet one more fork of aloo palak into his skinny frame.

"But you're moving people from where they were born; they've lived here relatively calmly for thousands of years. What a ridiculous notion to think they'll up sticks and move. Aren't most of the farmers around here Hindus? Are they supposed to just leave all their property and buildings?" Henry's passion became evident as he raised his voice. Hamilton and Watts exchanged amused glances.

"Come on, Henry, I think you have a vested interest here. A nice little doe-eyed beauty, maybe?"

"I wish you'd stop implying that Sunita is somehow more to me than she is. Yes, I think she is probably one of the most beautiful girls I've ever seen but that doesn't mean any more than that. Her family are honourable people, and as I said, have worked here for years."

"I'm surprised she's even allowed around us. Actually, wouldn't mind a bit myself if it came to it." Lieutenant Jones joined in after finishing his food, which he deemed far more important. "Thought about pulling her into a dark corner last week."

As the others laughed, Henry remained po-faced. He hated it when they started talking like this.

It offended him. He contemplated walking out as he had done earlier but stayed when he realised that the conversation had moved away from Sunita and on to fantasies of girls left behind, of conquests on previous leaves and the lure of the uniform.

"So, I says to her, you can blow on my buttons any time, darling; and she knelt down and started blowing. Well, if you get my drift, that's not all she blowed. I kept her address for a long time but last time I went back she'd moved; can't even remember her last name. Anyway, plenty more where she came from." Bob Jones leant back in his chair, the wicker pleading for his removal.

Henry tried to steer the conversation back to a political note, but the other men were into reminiscing and not interested in intelligent discussion. Henry felt that this might have had something to do with the copious amounts of wine they had consumed during the meal; and when Sunita's father came in to collect the plates with their remnants of curries now turned oily, they asked for even more.

"It's too hot in here. Let's go and sit outside," Henry ventured.

"Good idea. I'm getting a bit hot talking about Vanessa anyway." Bob heaved himself out of his chair, which sighed loudly at its release.

Chapter 9

1947

The night air was thick and sweet. The glow of their cigarettes lit up the veranda like so many fireflies. Henry sighed. The fans whirred loudly above their heads, stirring the stiff-leaved frangipanis drifting their night-time scent. It was usually Henry's favourite time of the day, the time he allowed himself to relax. The hustle and bustle of Peshawar, the crowded streets and thronging crowds all but vanished at night, especially since the imposition of the curfew; and here he was in a little oasis surrounded by scents and cooling breezes. Henry sighed again. He turned to join in the conversation, hoping to dispel his growing sense of disquiet. He heard chatter and clatter from the kitchen as the Mehras went about their daily chores, tidying up after dinner, soaking lentils for tomorrow and sweeping out the kitchen. He could hear the familiar swish of bristles on stone. Somehow, he didn't feel comforted.

George and John were laughing, and Bob was trying to keep a straight face as he described his efforts at talking Hindi in the bazaar.

'So I kept saying jildi, jildi and the poor man was so flustered wondering what he was supposed to be doing so quickly until I remembered it was jalebi I wanted. A few more confused moments and then he handed me one, dripping with syrup and I took it quickly, quickly." The others laughed again and finished their drinks.

"Talking of which," interrupted Henry, 'I'll go and ask if there are any in the kitchen."

John shook his head as Henry walked away. "He's got it bad. I bet you he won't be back for a while." They all laughed.

August 1947

My dear Patience,

Once again, I cannot tell you enough how much your letters mean to me. However oppressive the weather, however irksome my duties, they lift my spirit for days!

I am settling into the new duties which somewhat enables me to avoid thinking of all the atrocities around us and am quite enjoying all the ordering of items, at least the ones that we can order; still so many supplies in short supply as it were. How's the rationing going back home? My mother tells me that she's still finding it difficult to obtain even flour. Butter doesn't seem to be a problem as there are so many dairy farmers around and she can always rely on Mr Frampton, her pet shopkeeper, to find her some! I think she is feeling more herself these days and beginning to start organising her ladies' circle to raise money for the local orphans. She has even tried to involve Martha. I so want you to meet my sister next time I come home. You two would get along like a house on fire.

I manage to find a little time to read and you really must get hold of The Healing Knife by George Sava. It's quite an extraordinary story of his journey to being a surgeon. Wonderful stuff!

So, have you found anything more interesting to do with your time than going to the morgue? I do hope so. Write and tell me all.

As I read your letters I imagine you curled up by the fire reading them aloud, I hear your voice, see your smile and the odd little tooth you so hate, and I feel so good about the future! Rather bold, I know.

Thinking of you all the time,

Henry

August 1947

Dear Henry,

You are so naughty to send me those lovely white sandals. I don't know where you got them, but they fit perfectly and I do so love them. I don't know why you sent them; if only you knew what a worthless creature I am! I slept on and on this morning and if it hadn't been for the postwoman knocking on the door with the parcel, well, I might still have been asleep now. Anyway, it was a quarter to nine and gosh, did I have to fly! I just grabbed a piece of toast out of Max's hand as I passed through the kitchen and charged off to work and ate it there. I think I've been late every day this week; must start an early to bed movement!

You will be pleased to know that I have started art evening classes. I do so love them. I'll tell you more in my next letter.

Not so sure about The Healing Knife but I did like his Land fit for Heroes. Saw it in Boots the other day and thought of you. Would you like me to send it to you?

Have you heard: the Labour government are very cute? They have cut all interest on accounts in the banks! Just so you will find somewhere else to invest your money, like government loans and bonds. Clever – bank restraints – can't tell you how much we've lost but it's a good thing in a way; money will be put to good use instead of these bloated capitalists squirrelling it away! Ooh, singing the praises of Labour, boo hoo, you Tory!

Must push off now. Goodbye and keep safe.

Thank you again for my sandals, you dearest man, I can't thank you enough.

Yours affectionately,

Patience x

September 1947

My dearest Patience,

Once again, I have to say that I take such delight in hearing your tales of life back in Abergele. Please don't stop writing. I do enjoy every sentence.

Life here is busy. I am still busy procuring but it is very difficult as only the US seems to have anything left for us to use.

The weather here is getting cooler and we can parade around without any discomfort. I have even taken to putting on a pullover in the evening. Army issue of course.

Please write soon. I miss you and want to know every minute detail of what you do. A fortnight between letters seems an inordinate amount of time.

Give my regards to your mother and father and Max too.

Yours,

Henry

Dearest Henry,

So, you haven't had a letter from me for at least two weeks? Gosh, mail certainly takes a long time to reach you from here. But mail coming here from India is marvellous! Eight days usually. The letter you sent on the 9th of September arrived on the 17th.

Mummy has gone to a dinner tonight and I had to dash home in time to do her hair and give her that extra finishing touch which seems to give her confidence if I do it! What excitement, though, as this is quite a pukka peacetime affair!

I took my bike to the cycle shop today. You wouldn't recognise it. They've fastened up all the rattly bits and bobs, tightened screws and oiled this and that and for the crowning glory have put on a dynamo. I got caught by a copper the other evening for riding without a light. Usually, I manage to hop off in time and pretend to be pushing the bike but unfortunately, he was around a corner and certainly gave me what for. Now I can cycle to art class without slinking down Russell Street but pedal with marvellous satisfaction as I pass any policeman in the dark. I love the faint hissing noise the dynamo makes and how the faster you pedal the more insistent it becomes.

Mummy bought me a ticket to go to a dance tonight, but here I am sitting writing to you. I write so much more quickly when I am on my own in the house. Maybe it will take me about half an hour as opposed to the two to three hours it takes if there are others in the room.

There's a big dance in a fortnight, the Police Ball. There will be so many people to dance with and talk to. I'm quite excited about that one.

The other night I was reading Dragonwyck by Anya Seton, such a fabulous story, and decided I'd finish it in the bath. I ran a full and brimming one and settled in luxuriously to read. Max was stomping around the house looking for the book as he had got it out from the library. Eventually, he found out where I was and made periodic pilgrimages upstairs to tell me I'd been in an hour, then an hour and a half and when he got a bit wild at two hours, I thought I'd better shift! By then I'd finished the book anyway! I so enjoy reading and rush at it headlong and then skip passages. I don't have the time or patience (no pun intended) to read the book again.

Well, to explain my late reply, I go on strike on a Saturday. No letter writing by order of my union!

There's quite a constant murmur and a buzz about demob on these shores too. Have you heard any news? Usual speculations as to whether there is anything in the speed-up the government are chatting about.

As promised, more about my art classes. I rode through the rain the other night, nothing will stop me going, and hardly anyone was there. Bit challenging as we had to draw head and shoulders of our girl model looking down reading a book. Needed to think of foreshortening and all that. I'm learning so much and the two hours go by so fast. Then home with the dynamo. Fantastic!

That should be enough news to keep you going, you sweet man.

Cheerio and take care of yourself,

Patience x

October 1947

My dearest Patience,

My heart sings every time the post is dealt out and you do not know how it sags if there is no letter from you. How happy I was this time to receive two letters from you and a parcel.

You dear girl, sending me Land Fit for Heroes. I devoured it immediately and must admit it was a very interesting read; however, I do prefer The Healing Knife, maybe because I once felt the urge to study to become a doctor; not something I have ever told anyone before.

Everyone here is getting a bit skittish about wanting to know when they may be granted leave but at the moment they are keeping quite mum as the situation here is still on the boil. And of course, not even a whisper of any demob plans for us.

I cannot even begin to think of my return as it would make me feel very melancholy to think it might be so far away. Speaking of far away, it is your letters which keep me in touch with life at home and everything you are up to.

When we docked in Bombay, we were dispatched from a place called Deohlali which is a squalid, chaotic place. Luckily, we were only passing through. I felt sorry for those commissioned to remain in such madness. It's funny, though, as now we refer to anyone acting stupidly or manically as 'doolally'. Have you heard that? You could start using it and be quite up to date with a new expression.

That's all for now. I am on duty this evening.

Write to me as soon as you get this, I cannot wait longer.

Yours affectionately,

Henry

November 1947

Dearest Henry,

You silly man! You will have to wait for the post, you know it always takes longer when you are rushing to the mail sack every day. It's a bit like waiting for water to boil, isn't it?

My little news. I've been thinking that I will have a black suit made. Very smart and tailored with knife pleats at the back; but I'll have to wait until the next lot of coupons come out in March. Not sure if they will be enough though, only a measly twenty-four, I think. There really must be a terrific amount of black market going on when you look at all the suits and clothes women have. D'you think they think that of me?

There was quite an enjoyable play on 'Saturday Night Theatre' last night, His House in Order. We seem to do nothing but listen to the wireless these days as Max is on the BBC listening research panel. They send him all sorts of papers and questionnaire thingumabobs. He just revels in it and we do so enjoy giving scathing remarks about programmes like 'Music Hall' and 'The Old Town Hall'!

I went to tea with my friend Beryl the other day. I don't think you met her. She's about nine months younger than me and her husband darling is just 'in the army' and has no job prospects to come back to and this time next week he will be on board ship heading to your part of the world, I believe. Beryl's confidences on the wedding first night have not endeared me any more to marriage, just the opposite, they've made me plumb scared!

A letter arrived from that Scottish friend I met on a course ages and ages ago. Do you remember I told you he writes the silliest letters and poems to me? Well, he has been very unlucky. Did I tell you his fiancée got seriously involved with another chap and now after a period of silence from him of about five months he has written to say he was all lined up to marry someone else but she has pulled out with a fortnight to go? My goodness, imagine all the wedding preparations and everything. Now, whenever I see an envelope from him, I will wonder if he's on to fiancée number three!

It seems such a long time ago since you were here. Time passes so slowly in the winter.

Well, that's it for now, my darling, God bless and good night,
Patience xx

My dearest Patience,

Your talk of marriage fills me with hope. In all honesty, are you thinking about that? I am sure there is nothing to be frightened of. I would always treat you with kid gloves and respect. I really can't wait until we can be together. I'll share my thoughts and dreams with you as you are so perfect and will make me a much better man.

I only have a few minutes, so this will be very short but please know how much I care for you and about you.
Fondly yours forever,
Henry x

Patience ripped the envelope in half as she stood in the hallway. Marriage? She sighed as she looked at the other letters stacked on the hall table ready to be posted. Her boys. To Norman. To Richard. To Teddy. What had started as an earnest desire to help some of the troops abroad who had no one to write to had become a bit of a joke for her. She knew all their handwriting, the neat and the scrawly, and the many different coloured inks. She loved reading the sentiments they sent her, she loved receiving letters most days. And in her hand the letter from Henry. Oh. But marriage was furthest from her mind. Her frown deepened. Best forget about it for now and go and help her mother in the kitchen making cakes with the icing sugar Henry had so kindly sent.

"Patience, come on! You have the touch, the cool hands for pastry, you do. We only have an hour before the guests arrive."

Patience cast a glance at the pile of letters, blew a curl from her forehead, scuffed the toe of her shoe, and wondered if maybe she could still go to the pictures with Max if she got this chore done.

Chapter 10

November 1947

M y dearest Henry,
    I am sorry you got so carried away with my talk of weddings and marriage. No, I'm not considering marriage – leastways not any time soon! Not to you or anyone else, you silly goose! Don't be sad, I will still write to you. Who knows what will happen in the future, when you come home, when all the troops return?

Mummy and Daddy had a dinner party a few days ago and I was roped in to help with the cakes and pastry. Flattery goes a long way with me, and Mummy said my hands were perfect for making pastry so I made my celebrated cheese straws which went down a treat. I ended up making icing, too, for the cake. Thank you so much for sending the icing sugar; Mummy was very grateful.

Max and I were hoping to clear off to the pictures to see another James Mason film, but we were persuaded to stay for the dinner party and actually it was rather jolly although most of the guests were oldies. I did talk to a younger couple from Kimmel. A captain and his wife. Thought I'd keep in with them so they can let me know if there are any 'do's' on. We played some games although most of the oldies wanted to play sitting down games. We tried Wink, wink, murder but they didn't want to fall to the floor so that was a bit of a flop as it were, ha ha!

Dearest Henry, keep your chin up. It'll all be over soon.

Keep well and God bless,

Patience xx

Sitting on the veranda Henry sipped his gin and tonic. It was his third. Banter rose around and above him. He heard none of it. How had he mistaken her feelings? Since he had spotted her sitting behind the counter in the bank, a jewel, his feeling for her had always been a particular part of him, nurtured and held gently in his cupped hands. What did the endearments mean? The dearests and darlings? She had not spoken to him in soft words. It was only demonstrated in her letters which led to the belief of a stronger emotion which had elevated his hopes. Verandas inspire contemplation, their shade a safe thinking spot away from the outdoor glare.

Guffaws shot through his thoughts.

"Hey, Henry. Wakey, wakey!"

Henry shook his head. He rose and counted every step as he dragged himself back to his room. Sitting on the bed he glanced at his watch. Polishing shoes was the most important task, he thought. As he rubbed in the black polish he wondered if he had polished them already. Did it matter? The vigour and rhythm of the brush and the gentle hiss of the bristles soothed his jumpy mind so that it was dinner-time before he finished. A catatonic haze enveloped him. Two more letters from Patience piled up on his dresser unopened.

Henry looked at the leave forms in front of him. One caught his eye. Abergele, it said.

"Sergeant Edwards You're going to Abergele for your leave?"

"Yes, sir. I won the leave lottery. A whole month. Can't wait to see my girl."

"Lucky you." His laconic response implied no luck in the matter at all.

"Ah, sir. I'm right lucky. Patient I've been and now I'll get my reward. Patience will be waiting for me."

Henry stared at the lucky soldier.

"Patience, you say. Is that her name or what you've displayed?"

The soldier laughed.

"Yeah, sir, grand name, isn't it?" He pulled at his collar as he saw the horrified look on Henry's face.

"Sir?"

Before the soldier's eyes, Henry's face turned a mottled red, a vein pulsed in his temple. Sergeant Edwards watched in alarm as Henry pushed the table away from him, steadying it before it fell over. Henry smoothed his hair, patted it behind his neck.

"Look here, Jones!" He was yelling now. Soldiers in the line behind were looking on in bemusement. "If that's Patience Tarmaster, you've no right, no right at all!"

Edwards gaped.

"Yes, sir. I… I mean no, sir. Met her at the holiday camp last time I was at training. She didn't say anything..."

"She's my girl. My girl, do you hear? Don't you go anywhere near her, do you understand? That's an order!"

"Of course, sir. I didn't mean to upset you. I didn't know, sir. I honestly didn't."

Chapter 11

1947

No safe place now in the barracks: everyone would be sniggering and snickering at him. At least the veranda afforded him length to pace as his shoes squeaked their black shine back and forth. It was cruel. Life was cruel. He retired to his room and lay on the bed under the mosquito net, attempting sleep. The hours passed. He still felt the thrumming in his ears, his senses squeezed into one tiny part of his brain.

In the quiet of the deep night, gunshots rang out. Through his window, he saw a glow, unusual so early in the morning; and then came another shot, a gunshot not so far away. Henry dressed quickly and knocked on the other officers' doors.

"I think there's some trouble somewhere. Those bloody Pathans. Come on; get up. We'd better rouse the men. I'll go and tell the staff to stay put and not to venture out." Henry hurried along the corridor, the wooden floors hollow-sounding in the night.

He could hear hallooing and ululations in the distance. He hoped against hope there would be minimal bloodshed. But screams split the dark, tearing the stillness. He tried to remember what the doctor had said: breathe deeply. He threw open the kitchen door and practically tumbled down the stairs to the staff's outside quarters. The door to the sleeping area was wide-open. Crumpled sheets lay strewn on the ground;

haste had made the room untidy, drawers drooping, contents rifled through. But no sign of Sunita or any of her family. Henry felt panicked. Was that what had woken him up? Movement in the garden? He ran to the side entrance; that door too was wide open. Creaking on its hinges it swung to and fro.

Henry and John led their men down the street by the houses on Main Road following the sounds of raised voices, the harsh shattering of glass and the hubbub of louder crashes and splintering punctuated by cheering. As they rounded the corner into Qissa Khwani, flames greeted their eyes and smoke hindered their vision. A confused melee of tribesmen sporting turbans and rifles were butting the shop fronts. Dark shapes shifted and ran away down the alley at the side, followed immediately by howls and stampeding feet.

John spoke. "I'm not sure what we should do. Orders were to stay out of it. Let the Pathans settle their scores."

"Well, I'm not standing by, John. Come on."

They followed the crowd down the laneways towards the main bazaar. A pile of rubble lay where the rock wallah had left it. Bright coloured awnings reached across the narrow alleyways. Turbans and knives; flashes of colour and glint of steel preceded them. In the breaking light, a thin stream of smoke curled from a nearby rooftop. Henry hoped vainly that it was a morning cooking fire. His heart stretched his chest, clamouring to be let out before it burst with anxiety. He licked his dry lips, tasting a heady mixture of sweat and smoke. John was running close behind him.

Suddenly they stopped, as a nearby scream

snapped their nerves. An army-like grey coldness descended and both John and Henry's training took over. Henry moved as in a mist. Shapes in the clearing gloom surrounded two black piles of cloth. Lust and fever threaded themselves through the looming bodies, ancient enmities streaming down blow after blow. A deadly pounding rhythm of hatred and bloodletting.

Henry felt indomitable as he heard the familiar thud of booted soldiers racing behind him. He charged forward, buoyed by authoritarian shouts, to confront the tribesmen. The leader turned and faced the soldiers, crazed, glazed eyes blinking dark with animosity.

The thudding in Henry's ears drove out all sensible thought. He lurched forward to the black piles on the ground. Surprised, the tribesmen moved apart to let him pass. A sudden yell came from the alleyway behind them. The tribesmen hallooed, raised their faces to their gods, brandished their guns and knives and took off.

"No!" ordered Henry. "Don't follow them; help me here."

He knelt and very gently peeled back a layer of shroud black as it lay on a bed of crushed glass and frangipani blossoms. The sweetest scent at the cruellest hour. His ears buzzed with the rush of blood; wave upon wave of nausea rose as he gently stroked the delicate skin. Carefully he placed a hand under Sunita's head. It felt hot; was she still breathing? Her arm fell lifelessly as he picked her up, her bangles tinkling mischievously, denying the fact of her death, reaching, reaching, plucking heaven's mangoes.

"Fetch a stretcher. I think her father is still breathing." John crouched over the mangled form, over the blood-drenched cloth.

The cowardly night was over; sun slants over the rooftops made their way into the bazaar. The sound of shouting was now distant. The tribesmen were leaving, running away to the hills until they descended again to even another score.

Chapter 12

April 1948

Dear Henry,
I'm not sure whether I should even call you 'dear'. I am so furious. How could you have told Richard he was not to see me? I am not 'your girl'. I am no-one's girl and I have a good mind not to write to you again.

It's just my luck that he had to come to you about his leave – you would never have known otherwise, although there is nothing to know, it's so innocent.

I haven't heard from you for months, so I suppose you are mad with me too. Well, I think you are 'doolally'. So at least I have learnt something from you, if only a word.

I may or may not see you when you finally come over. I am fuming.
Patience

April 1948

Dear Patience,
I feel very aggrieved. I feel that you led me on. If you could read back your letters you would see why I thought as I did. My life is empty without

you and your letters. I don't think you understand what it is like to be stationed here. To live amidst all the tension and violence.

I don't think you realise how much I depended on taking those small stories of your everyday life and putting them carefully away in my pocket to think about later, in those moments of calm, sitting here on the veranda ignoring gunshots and screams. I wished I was part of your life. The most important part of it, the one you wanted to come home to. The one who would encourage you to draw, to paint, to leave your stultifying job. I wanted to be the one to see you grow, to be by your side, to smell your beautiful skin, to love all of you.

Don't write to me unless I write to you. I am licking my wounds. I had opened my heart to someone who was not ready to receive it. I am embarrassed. I am fuming too.

Henry

"God, those fellows are noisy!"

"Well, Henry, I for one would much rather they let off steam here than running around the bazaar after women or beating up little old men who crossed their path," rejoined Captain John Watts.

Henry held his gin and tonic against his cheek, the condensation cool as he watched the antics. Two of the young scouts on leave from the remote tribal areas were egging on another, pale and ginger-haired, who was riding round and round the pool on a bicycle. Eventually all three of them, laughing and slithering about, picked up the bike and started hauling it laboriously up the diving board steps.

"What on earth are they up to now?" Henry closed his eyes as the whooping and yells of encouragement became louder. His stomach clenched. He felt a lurch in his guts. He opened his eyes to see that the bicycle was now perched precariously on the diving board with one scout holding it for the other to climb onto, his red hair on fire, a beacon, a fiery contrast to the sweating white skin.

"They'll kill themselves."

"I think they're too drunk for that, Henry. He'll probably wind himself, though, as he hits the water."

They both watched in amazement as the soldier pedalled full pelt along the diving board, wavering and wobbling. In the air, he separated himself from the bike and dived away until he finally hit the water followed closely by the bike. The others roared and clapped appreciatively. He emerged from the water with one fist raised triumphantly. He shook his head, spraying cooling drops of water before diving to retrieve the trusty cycle.

"Top marks, Pete!"

"Hang on. I can do better than that."

A small wiry soldier, who had been shading his eyes, swayed slightly and started to run toward the steps to the diving platform. The others laughed. He stumbled and almost fell but turned around and grinned at his fellow soldiers.

"I'm all right. I can do it. I can do it."

Someone shouted, "Have another drink." He shook his head, the effort of which nearly made him fall again; but grasping the handrails of the diving board he pulled himself up one stair at a time, missing his footing at every other rung.

"Bloody fool. He shouldn't be trying anything, the state he's in. This is their last day here, isn't it? Thank god the club will return to normal tomorrow."

"Until the next leave of course," added Henry.

Draining the last of his gin, Henry stood up to go. He looked at the surrounding soldiers shouting to the man on the board who, it seemed clear from commands and gesticulation, was planning to jump from the high platform onto the diving board and then into the pool.

"For god's sake, will someone stop him? He'll kill himself, John." Henry stood up and strode towards them. "Hey, get down from there. Enough of that now."

But it was too late. The soldier had launched himself, falling clumsily onto the springboard which reacted to his weight and propelled him at great speed off the board, the trajectory determined by the soldier's inaccurate jump. His body, a clumsy bag of flailing limbs, fell onto the grass surrounding the pool. The thud and the ensuing groans silenced the shouts of encouragement. The malis attending the deckchairs, sweeping and cleaning around them, froze in the silence. The fountains remained oblivious and continued their splashing and tinkling, displaying an incongruous levity.

Suddenly everything jerked into action. The malis and bearers rushed to the scene; the soldiers clustered around the broken moaning man. Henry yelled at one of the bearers to rush inside and telephone for the medics. The soldier was sprawled widely, his white skin vivid against the dusty grass. Henry noticed the brown lines around his neck, his arms, his ankles: rings of colour, brown skin against white, a chocolate and vanilla nursery pudding. One of his legs was twisted at an unnatural angle. He was a human swastika, its blessings of safety and happiness far from him.

Chapter 13

August 1948

Dear Patience,
It has been a while since I wrote, as of course you know, and I miss your news.

It has been pretty horrendous here and I need the vision of your sweet face to comfort me. We have still not heard anything about demob; such a long job here with the aftermath of partition. I'm sure I've talked about it before, but it is so complicated and a situation I would rather be out of.

Everyone is getting very jittery and misbehaving badly when they get the chance. Some fellow playing the fool last week got himself badly hurt by trying to dive off a board into the pool at the Peshawar club, with a bicycle, would you believe?

How are your art classes? I am sure that you will be quite the artist by the time I return and will have gone very bohemian, with overalls and spatters of paint everywhere. Have you given any more thought to a change of career? How is your father reacting to you attending classes? I suppose he doesn't mind as he doesn't see this as a threat to your bank work. If you asked again about going to art college he might think differently?

I don't want to talk about what happened. I

hope you won't either.
Henry

Henry could not believe what he was writing. Not talk about it? It had consumed his every waking thought for months. As he woke in a sweat, the stifling mosquito net preventing even the faintest of breezes, his first thought was of Patience. Her soft skin, the tiny chip on her front tooth which she said Elsie had caused by tipping a glass bottle of pop too vigorously against her mouth. He loved it all. He would write today. But another day went by and he couldn't find the words. Those he managed to dredge out were transparent and rattled around on the page saying nothing. Saying nothing of his shredded heart, of the faithlessness of his chosen one. He folded the letter many times before placing it in the wastepaper basket beneath his desk.

After the violence of the night the Pathan tribesmen descended into the marketplace from the hills, his heart had been squeezed. Sunita's death had left it in a desiccated state. He needed Patience to inject some life into it, to plump it up to a functioning organ, to wipe away the horrors. He retrieved the letter from the basket and, sighing, smoothed it out.

Chapter 14

October 1948

Dear Henry,

My, my, that was a surprise, hearing from you after all this time. I truly thought you would never write again, my sweet. No, I must limit my blandishments. Is that the right word?

You say nothing about your duties. Are you going to do any survey work? I know at one time that is where you thought they would use you after your training at Larkhill, so you said. But I suppose it's not so useful now that fighting has finished. Or has it, where you are? The BBC mentions how tricky things are in India in general. I worry and of course, Father eagerly scans the papers to find out anything from back home.

It is getting cold here and I sit and watch leaves twirling and swirling through the bank window. I sit as the front teller, to have a better view, not that there's too much to see, as you know.

It has been quite quiet here as far as dances go. There is one this weekend at the Queen's Hotel, but I don't think I'll go as I don't know anyone who is going and there's nothing more boring than not having someone to talk to or dance with.

Ooh, some news. Max and Elsie are no longer stepping out and Max, of all people, decided to join the Navy! I can't believe it. Neither can Daddy; he is furious, as you can imagine. Max didn't tell him until he had signed up and found out that he was accepted. Daddy hasn't got any energy left to worry about my art classes as he worries daily about Max who has almost finished his training and embarks soon for heaven knows where. Perhaps he will come out to your neck of the woods. I will let you know if I hear anything. Not much chance, though; he keeps mum about these things.

I think that's all the news for now.

Fondly yours,

Patience

November 1948

Dear Patience,

I am glad we can write to each other civilly. I think it is for the best if you keep the endearments to a minimum. I will endeavour to do the same.

It was quite a shock to hear about Max. You didn't mention what your mother thought about it? I expect your father will be trying all he can to extricate him. It will be hard; do you know how long he has signed on for? You must be missing him too and your house will be all the quieter.

Yours in haste for the post,

Henry

December 1948

Dear Henry,

Thanks for your letter which I received so quickly after the last one. Are you lonesome or something? Sorry, couldn't resist a dig after the sudden renewal of your lagging correspondence.

Well, I'm almost roasted alive. It is so darn cold outside that I thought I would stoke up a lovely fire. Jeepers, it is now so hot, I can see myself and my chair moving further and further away from those cheery flames.

Mummy has trotted off to Ye Olde Timers, probably to stop her thinking about Max and the perils he might be facing. I know, I know, the war is over, and we are soon to have our second Christmas of peace, but where you are it seems to be getting worse. Daddy has read out some terrible things about Peshawar and he despairs of any news of his family.

Perusing proofs of portraits I have had taken at the photographer's in Rhyl I am surprised how bad they are. I tried not to smile so I didn't show my tooth, but it has lent me a sinister, lopsided look. On the wall of the photographer's there is a plaque which says, 'Satisfaction Guaranteed'. I told her that I was not satisfied, and she has agreed to take them again. I was going to send you one but really, they are awful.

You will be pleased to know that I have clamped down on being sentimental and now burn your letters after I have answered them.

I went to Manchester the day after I last wrote to you. They are slowly getting more and more goods in the shops. I told myself off severely for succumbing to a white sweater and a pair of black suede gloves. I went with the firm intention of buying only Xmas presents but I did need the black gloves for my black suit, and you can't wear anything but suede with a dressy suit, can you? The white sweater is not quite Lana Turner-ish but cute all the same.

I came home to find Max here. He had been given some time off before he leaves. He told me that he is courting again. Someone called Joyce who is also in the Navy in the Women's Auxiliary. I think he wanted to bring her to meet Mummy and Daddy but of course, it would have been too lucky for them to have the same days off! We shall wait and see.

Been to a few films, nothing very good. Smoky and No Leave, No Love – terribly overrated.

I'm going to The Grand in Llandudno this week to see The Wind and the Rain; it's due in London next month. We are fortunate to see them before they hit the West End.

Gee, think of it, it'll soon be Xmas. I know you once thought you'd be home for this one, didn't you? I think this new demob programme stinks. Well, it does. At least they could give you some leave.

That's it. You can get on with your day's work as if I'd never interrupted it.
Yours,
Patience

Chapter 15

Rhyl, November 1949

It was a bitter morning. A good day for letter-writing. With Shadow the cat seated comfortably on her knees, purring now and then – a black hot water bottle – Patience looked over her letters.

Her correspondents were dwindling. They had all found their lives again. They had returned to Wales, England or even Scotland and drifted off, back to being bankers, publishers and accountants. Even Henry. On returning from India he had not visited her. He obviously hadn't forgiven her. He had taken up where he left off at university before enlisting in the war but had changed his subject to journalism. Patience wondered whether he would write about India; expunge from his memory the atrocities tangled with the vibrancy and immediacy of a country which he had loved.

Max had not stayed long in the Navy; he was now the proud owner of Welsh Heather, a company which made soaps and perfumes. Max had run into Henry on a recent sales trip to Bath. He said that Henry was moving further down south, to Dorchester, he believed. Henry was astonished to see him, he said. He had, of course, asked after Patience: what she was doing, who she was seeing; but carelessly, casually, as if he held no further desire in his heart. He had got married, shortly after returning, to a wonderful woman, he stressed, whom he had met at a publishing house; Mary was her name; and they were relocating to Dorset because her family lived there and as he would soon be a father, it would be good for Mary to be near the encircling arms of her parents and the comfort they could provide. Confidences he would not normally have divulged tumbled out of him. Henry cherished privacy, revealing little to his acquaintances; and it surprised him how vehemently he wanted to impress the importance of his new relationship upon Max, how important he felt it was for Max to understand.

Henry gave Max his new address just in case he happened to go to Dorchester, although he understood his sales territory was nowhere in the South.

All this Patience mulled over.

There was dear old Gordon. He still wrote to her regularly. A childhood friend; he drivelled on about people she knew and people she didn't. Her parents liked Gordon. They liked his family. They liked his prospects: an accountant in his father's accounting firm. They felt that she should marry him. Not on your nelly! Endless days and boring nights, she thought, were not for her. Conversation with no spark, no discussion of books – he didn't like reading – no dances, parties or flirtations. She could see her life with him stretching into a meaningless existence. But her mother would ask if she had written back to him. The letters arrived monotonously, on alternate days, except for Mondays when she was likely to receive two. Predictable.

She thought of Henry. How angry she had been when he had tried to contain her, to possess her, to curb her letter-writing, to stop her seeing who she wished to see. Gordon would never have done that. He would have smiled at her and said, of course, you can write to whom you like. She began to think of herself as a brightly coloured butterfly. Taking the sweetness when she could, avoiding the dull blooms, the withering, the faded and the blown.

Dear Gordon…

Part II

Chapter 16

Rhyl, May 1950

Arm in arm, Elsie and Patience strolled through the gates to the holiday camp. Just like the old days. Patience eyed up the dance hall. Some locals she recognised; she returned their smiles without much enthusiasm. She turned to Elsie and pulled down the corner of her mouth. Elsie laughed then nudged Patience with her elbow. There in the corner. A young man with upswept black hair and a dapper moustache.

The two girls paused. He glanced in their direction with a hint of a smile, recognition that he was being watched. He adjusted his shirtsleeves exposing achingly white cuffs with a glint of dazzling blue cufflink. His jacket was straight from London; Patience had only seen the like of it in magazines. His style singled him out for attention, it even danced around his baggy brown corduroy trousers with their upturned cuffs.

"Joe, come on. We're ready to start when you are," another dapper-dressed band member called out to him.

The young man turned on his heel – no scuffs, Patience noted – and took his place behind the drum kit.

A live band. The makings of a jolly evening. Patience and Elsie danced. They danced to old tunes, they danced to tunes that had not yet reached Wales, they danced until their shins ached. Patience watched the deft drum-strokes out of the corner of her eye. Elsie waved at her, her grin showing: I know what you're looking at.

He was so different from anyone she had known before. He had not completed his architectural studies; he had entered the world of construction in London, preferring the physical challenge over the meticulous detailing. Just up on holiday, helping his brother who owned the camp. A London spiv, her father said.

"He's not a professional. I hope you have no serious intentions." And of course, she did have. She felt compelled.

It was a whirlwind courtship. He thrilled her; he was so different from all those young men who had passed through her life. He did not set out to impress. One day while playing table tennis at the club he crouched down, twisted his face into a Frankenstein, held his arms to his chest and limped after Patience, dragging one foot behind him. Patience gasped. Had he gone mad? Was he insane? She shrieked; her heart pounded until he pounced and, laughing, they fell onto the floor.

Chapter 17

1951 to 1954

After the wedding Patience and Joe moved to a tiny flat in a nearby town and horrified both her father and mother by mixing concrete for a pathway Joe was laying.

"He's not good enough for you. Why didn't you marry Gordon or even Henry? I don't understand you," her father said on one of his visits when he swept in with Mother in tow. His knowing eyes took in the frayed cushions, the faded curtains.

In 1953 a baby girl was born, and Joe took off to Scotland. 'A great opportunity' to be a site manager on a hydroelectric scheme in the Highlands.

"Stay with us," said her parents. "We will look after you and the baby. Don't go up there. It is too wild and remote."

She went. She lived in a stone cottage, damp seeping through the walls into her heart. The sadness of Culloden Moor, the very bleakness of it crept under the sills; and her spirit withdrew, curled up to keep itself warm as she added another log to the fire, its flames telling her stories.

And Henry? After the birth of his second daughter, he and his wife moved back to Bath. Max had seen him. Walking through Bath, between Timothy White's and Boots on the High Street, Max noticed a tall man striding along on the other side of the road. His way of setting his feet down with such purpose made Max look at him. He took in the excessively shiny shoes and the Fair Isle sweater over a starched collared shirt and recognised the man out of uniform.

"Henry!" he called and lifted a hand in greeting.

News was exchanged and in his next telephone call to Patience, Max was able to relay the information Henry had given him with such eagerness. He was moderately successful having taken over his wife's family company, printing small editions of essays and political pamphlets.

"Come for dinner, old chap. About seven? We can reminisce. – Do you have any recent photos of Patience?"

The only one that Henry had, tucked in the back of his wallet, well-thumbed, was the studio portrait of Patience that she had sent him so many years ago. The one that she didn't like that showed her uneven, chipped tooth, the tooth that gave her the slightly less than perfect look.

Amongst his samples for the chemists, Max kept a few photos in his briefcase. One was of his wife Lucy and their two sons, smiling cheerfully as they built a sandcastle on the beach. His wife, her blonde hair tied back with a red-spotted scarf he had bought her the last time he was in Swansea, cradled his younger son in one arm whilst helping the elder turn out a bucket onto the very pinnacle of the mounded sand.

The other photo he kept was one that his father had taken. His mother stood, awkwardly squinting in the sun, her focus on Patience who was holding a squirming child against the backdrop of a Scottish loch. Your gaze followed the contours of the hills surrounding the loch into the highlands behind. It was grey and misty.

He handed the photo to Henry who scrutinised the small figures.

"Sorry," Max said, "Father's not so good at taking photos. More of the scenery than the family!"

"But is she happy?" he demanded.

Max wasn't sure of the answer to this and said, "Let's talk more this evening. I'll be happy to come to your house. Around seven you said?"

Max and Henry talked. Henry had forgotten how much he had enjoyed Max's company. Not just his closeness to Patience but his bright outlook on life. He learnt that when Max left the Navy, he had spurned a return to the accountancy future his father had laid out for him. He did not wish to follow a straight road; he preferred one with hedges, curves and surprise vistas around every corner. Elsie, his first love, had not taken to the new Max. She had envisaged a safe route in life; she did not like change. Max shook off the loss of Elsie as soon as he was in the Navy, had a brief affair with Joyce which did not end amicably and then met Lucy almost immediately afterwards, a vivacious, carefree spirit with springy blonde hair and an upturned nose. An effervescent twinkle caused Max to laugh in her company and very shortly he announced to his parents that he would be married on his next leave home.

Max found Henry's wife Mary to be a quiet, self-contained person who did not offer any insights into her life or relationship with Henry. She fussed in the kitchen before and after the meal, only joining them shortly before Max left. She sat on the sofa, knees primly turned to one side as Henry talked about Italy, about the almost derelict villa he had inherited from a cousin on his mother's side, in the town where his mother spent her early years. Max noted the disinterest on Mary's face, how she picked at fluff on her cardigan sleeve, how she avoided eye contact with either Henry or Max.

Chapter 18

1955 to 1995

Over the next forty years, Henry and Max exchanged periodic phone calls or bumped into each other accidentally or by design. After a while, Max stopped updating Patience. She rarely returned to Wales to visit her parents or brother, but followed Joe and his career around the UK and then on short contracts to Saudi Arabia, then Barbados and the Cayman Islands. She was struggling in her marriage and didn't want to worry her family.

In 1963 the world of art college seemed a faraway goal. It would be, after all, Patience's first foray into total independence, conviction in herself, faith in where her talents lay. As Patience's desire for independence grew, so did Joe's neediness. It was a given that she would be at home cooking dinner for him, that she would be there when the girls returned from school, that she would do the ferrying to and from ballet lessons, gymnastics and music.

"If you want to go to college, you will just have to fit it all in. I'm not coming home early to be there; I can't. The sites are too far away. I spend all day driving as it is, visiting and managing disasters. It's not an easy job, you know. Remember, it's my career that lets you live like this."

She had heard it before. She turned her back on

him, walked away and made a lemon surprise pudding, the familiar recipe and the beating motion a rhythm to her brain, to her desires. As the citrus tang wafted out of the oven, she remembered the interview she had had with the director of the art college.

"You are aware, I presume, being a mature student, that you must work harder than the students coming straight out of school. I know you're keen, I've no doubt about that, but with a young family…"

"It's something I've always wanted. I told you how my father didn't agree to send me to art college before, when I was young. But I know I can do it."

"Well, I hope your husband is happy with this decision?"

"Oh, yes, of course, he is so proud of me for passing the entrance exam. He'll do all he can to help."

Which of course he didn't. It was an uphill battle, a road paved with boulders, gravel in the shoes, lumps in her tomato soup; but eventually, she became an earner, a primary school teacher with an art speciality. It was good. She blossomed; once again she felt that she could do almost anything. There was a shine to her eyes, her figure was leaner, her wit more acute. It was now that she felt she could stand side by side with her husband, sometimes stepping forward; but he did his best to yank her back, to sink her confidence, to submerge it under his cutting cruelty, humour thrown over it like a faint gauze.

Max intuited but little of this on her flying visits back home, but unconsciously he must have imparted a suspicion to Henry. Henry was concerned. He had worries of his own as the caring for his wife became more and more intense. But this was a distraction. This was a situation of which he felt in control, purely because it was a fantasy. A dream of his to keep wrapped in tissue and golden string, to take out in the quiet of a sleepless night and smile at, with a wistful gaze, a future imagined where he would encourage and support. A dream reimagined from so long ago.

Henry's wife Mary was now in a wheelchair, the result of a car accident when their girls were seven and ten. She had retreated into her private world where no one could reach her; she showed even less love for or interest in either Henry or the girls and stared out of the bay window at the passing pedestrians, becoming animated only when a dog went past. Her smile would fade as soon as it disappeared, and her eyes would fix again on an invisible point in the distance. Henry spent more and more time in the printing office.

On her mother's death, Patience relented on her decision not to venture to Australia where Joe's two eldest brothers had emigrated. It was there, at her furthest distance from him, that Henry resolved to make personal contact with her.

Part III

Chapter 19

June 1995

Coincidences are such an important part of life, Henry thought, when he discovered through Max that Patience's youngest daughter was now living in East Devon, not so far from Dorchester where he still travelled to see his very aged in-laws, taking Mary who sat in her wheelchair and looked through both her parents, who sat eager for any scrap of recognition from her.

He had left her at her parents' nursing home, wondering again whether that was where she too should be admitted. He drove along the A35, up hill and down dale indeed, he thought, as field after field unrolled before him, veering away from the Roman road, down into a village with a busy stream alongside, swollen to bursting by the recent heavy rains.

He remembered walking with Patience through the Botanic Gardens in Bath, the combes rolling away before them, so green, lush and luxuriant, fresh from the evening's heavy rain. He touched Patience on her shoulder as he pointed out a hawk circling high above them. She frowned as she squinted, trying to make out the shape hovering, hovering.

He patted his hair, smoothing the strands, tucking in the strays at his collar.

Dear Matilda,

This is very presumptuous of me, I know, and I will quite understand if you do not wish to meet me.

I am an old friend of your mother's. We knew each other when we were very young in Wales at the end of the war.

Your Uncle Max told me that you were now living in Axminster and I would very much like to see you for tea and have a chat about your mother. I am going to be in Dorchester on family business on the 17th of this month and could meet you at The Bull Hotel, Bridport, a halfway point as it were, at 11 am if that would be convenient.

I look forward to hearing back from you.

Yours sincerely,

Henry Parker

Matilda telephoned her mother immediately. She wasn't due to phone for ten days but this, she felt, was an exception.

"Mummy, who is this fellow? Such a strange letter. Do you think I should meet him? What could he want to say?"

Her mother told her very little.

"Ah, Henry. Yes, he was somewhat sweet on me back then. But fancy him getting in touch with you. How on earth did he find out where you were?"

"Through Uncle Max. But I'll tell you more after I've seen him if you think it's okay. He's not some creepy old pervert, is he?"

Her mother laughed.

"I think it will be just fine. Well, well, dear old Henry! I don't think you should mention this to your father though…"

"Why ever not? I'm only going to have a cup of tea with him…"

Matilda sat at the scrubbed pine table, tracing intricate old woodworm pathways in between glances towards the door and the street life passing by. She wanted to size him up before he caught sight of her. He had said he would wear a carnation in his buttonhole. Buttonhole! Who has a buttonhole these days?

It was five to eleven as a very tall elderly gentleman, with greying hair swept up to give volume over some encroaching bald patches and wearing an immaculately pressed navy-blue blazer, opened the door and peered into the gloom. Matilda appraised his hawk nose and upright bearing. A pink carnation on his lapel confirmed her assumption.

She stood up and stepped forward, dropping the menu to the ground as she did so. An embarrassing tussle ensued as they both stooped to retrieve it.

Matilda held out her hand and Henry took it in both of his, shaking it up and down, clasping it between bony, dry palms.

"I can't quite believe it," he said; "you look so much like your mother. Not her colouring, of course, but certainly those dark eyes. I can even see her smile."

Matilda felt overcome by the scrutiny and nervously extracted her hand and gestured for him to sit down.

It was an awkward meeting, all in all. Matilda was not sure how to respond to Henry's insistent questioning. He allowed no interest in his own family or life; it was all about her mother.

He rubbed his manicured hands together, his shiny nails winking as he leant in towards her.

She didn't like his smile; too unctuous, she thought, demanding to be liked.

"I would like to contact your mother," he pleaded. "It's been too long…"

He saw Patience once again as she tapped a shiny toe at the bottom of his parents' stairs, her black jacket enlivened by the orange scarf he had bought her, soft silk against black curls, her generous smile highlighted by the cheeky dimple at the side of her mouth. She looked past him to her brother and Elsie tripping down, the old stairs creaking

"Come on, you two, Henry and I are waiting. You take so long to get ready!"

Henry shook his head, eyes focused on Matilda sitting in front of him; not Patience.

"I don't know," Matilda replied. "I will have to ask her."

"I can ask her if you give me her address… Well, I have a letter to her here, you know; perhaps you would like to send it with one of your own and then she can write back to me if she likes."

The latter seemed the less harmful of the two options. Harmful: why was she thinking this? She felt uneasy. It was his soft voice, wheedling almost, that made her stand abruptly and say, "I have to go and pick up my daughter from school early today. She has a music lesson at another school. I'm sorry, I must leave now, or I'll be late."

Somehow, though, she found she had the letter in the fire engine red pocket of her coat as she left the hotel, shutting the door rather too loudly in her hurried exit.

Besotted. Silly old fool.

"Mummy, do you realise he remembered every item of clothing you ever wore? Well, it certainly seemed like it. I couldn't believe it – what a funny old fellow. I think he's more than sweet on you."

"Oh, I think it's just for old times' sake, Matty; it was such a long time ago."

"Well, he wants to write to you. I've even got a letter here to send you. No, I haven't read it. Should I? What should I tell him? He's waiting to hear. He's coming back down to Dorset in a few weeks, he said."

"Oh, darling, I don't know. Send it on. I suppose it couldn't do any harm, could it?"

Chapter 20

July 1995
New South Wales,

Patience felt a flutter, a peculiar squeezing of her stomach; a giggle arose. It was a long time since she had written letters to one of her 'admirers'. Who would have thought it at this time of her life?

She looked in the mirror and impatiently tidied a curl. Still such dark hair. Wrinkles of course, and those ghastly shadows under her eyes. She pulled down her golf shirt and turned sideways to glance at the slim figure. A little pull-in of the stomach, a squint of the eyes and she could be getting ready for a holiday camp dance. She almost skipped down the stairs, humming as she went into the kitchen to prepare dinner.

August 1995
Bath

> My dearest Patience,
>
> I cannot tell you how pleased I am to be writing to you again. I have every one of your letters you ever sent me. See, I didn't burn them like you did!
>
> Do you remember saying 'You are so sensitive, you take any little thing I say to heart'? I am not so sure that I have changed much. Any

compliment or sweet expression from you will buoy me up for days.

Mary is going into respite care for a few weeks and I shall take the opportunity to go to Italy, to my villa. It's rather in need of some restoration, like myself, but I do so feel at home there. My cousins make me feel very welcome and prepare the best of Italian food. I will sit and think of you as I sip my chianti and take in the smell of the mountain pines which loom over the back of the house.

I remember coming here and standing on the cool flagstones in the kitchen while my Nonna rolled out pasta on the table. She sent me out to feel under the chickens for eggs; and how I disappointed her if I returned empty-handed because I was afraid of being pecked! Once the pasta was boiling for supper and the tomatoes simmering, she took me on her knee and sang sweet lullabies.

It was always warm there, golden light flooding the courtyard and out onto the cobbled alleyways where Silvia, my cousin, and Giovanni, the baker's son, played marbles endlessly. It was not easy playing marbles on cobbles and I invariably lost.

This time I am not losing. I will feel like a young man again. Excited and happy, twigs in my hair as I chop down the bushes at the side of the house to let in more of that golden sunshine that I remember.

I will write to you from San Cassiano.

Yours, always,

Henry

Chapter 21

April 1996
Devon

Matilda folded the girls' laundry into the wicker basket ready to take upstairs. She smoothed the green uniform skirts and white blouses. Holding a leotard in her hands, she buried her face in its crumpled scent and stared out of the window at the lime-green beeches unfurling their spring glory. A 'go-between'. She was unsure of her suitability for this role. She had read too many stories, followed too many film narratives where this role was a preface to a disastrous event, a calamity, a mighty moral upheaval. Her father had always encouraged her to do what she wanted. To attend university, to follow a career; but the modern outlook he felt he showed was limited. You could always be a bilingual secretary, but never a diplomat or a translator for the United Nations. She remembered the giddy nerves as she stood at the start of her gymnastics floor routine, waiting for the familiar notes of 'Congratulations' to start as she showed off her moves. Showed off to whom? Her father never came to see her; he said he was proud, but he never walked into the halls to see her. She had tried so hard to be the model daughter but her partner choices had not earnt any respect from either her mother or father. Despite all, she loved her father and felt uneasy about any kind of deception. How to explain this odd feeling, a kind of frisson about this reinstatement of love interest in her mother? She had recently heard the term 'moral compass'. She knew what her sister Beth would say. Many a night she lay awake in her double bed, looking out at the stars, wondering in which direction her compass should point.

The letters from Henry were arriving regularly and she forwarded them on to her mother. Her mother was increasingly girlish on the phone.

"So, what does he write about, Mummy?"

"Oh, not much really. Do you know he completed a journalism degree in his late thirties after he struggled with keeping the printing business going? I think it was a distraction from looking after Mary and the girls."

Another time she said, "We're just catching up; such a lifetime ago."

And then, "I think I might see him when I come over to see you next summer."

"Oh, Mummy, do you think you should?"

The letters continued in a torrent. On a visit to Dorset, he arrived uninvited at Matilda's cottage across the border in Devon, a giant in the small doorway, stooping to enter and fold his long frame into the Queen Anne chair by the fire.

"I wanted to send your mother something for Christmas but I'm not sure how to do it."

He pulled a small box from his pocket. Blue marbled paper, a nest of cotton wool. A thin looped gold chain with a small charm, a distinctive red coral Italian corno fastened with intricate golden filigree. With a hesitant smile, he drizzled it into Matilda's outstretched hand.

She looked at the serpentine twining and the

exquisite workmanship.

"It's beautiful," she breathed.

"Historically, it's very symbolic in Italy," he explained; "it's supposed to guard against the evil eye, but I can't think that your mother will need it for that!"

She took custody of the gift. She ran through various scenarios of how to send this necklace away from the prying eyes of the customs officer and – more importantly – from her father.

Sent simply as a present from her would be out of character. It was not the kind of design she favoured either for herself or her mother. She could not state its value in a parcel and could not afford the insurance needed for its safe passage through regular postal channels. She could pretend that it was only a piece of costume jewellery she had picked up at a charity shop; but again, it would show as jewellery and might be scrutinised by a canny customs officer.

She opened a packet of anti-static tumble dryer sheets and wrapped them carefully around the necklace. She replaced the sheets and glued back the end tabs. A strange present to receive, surely, but one that would not be suspected of containing anything so expensive or decorative. Her mother had previously commented that she had not seen dryer sheets for sale in Australia – an American invention, probably; but of course, there was little need for them, as the abundant sunshine did a far better job than any machine. But it was quirky and much more in keeping with a present that she might send. Her mother and father would laugh and say: typical Matty!

Next step was alerting her mother to the hidden treasure and that she needed to open up the box in private. Not even in front of her sister, who she knew without asking would adamantly oppose this subterfuge.

Matilda wondered how her mother would explain such an intricate piece. But once safely arrived at its destination that would be the end of her role. How her mother chose to explain it away would be up to her. She was an exceptional storyteller and should have no difficulty. Matilda thought back to the nights cuddled with her sister, under the blue-flowered eiderdown she had so loved, with her arm snaking over her sister's shoulders, pleading with her mother for yet another chapter in the Peter and Molly stories she would weave: a reflection of their own daily lives with a pinch of adventure and much love. The sisters would beg their mother for more; and one day after school, as they walked hand in hand through the back door, she presented them with an illustrated version of her tales. The line drawings, meticulous and frivolous at the same time, added a dimension to the stories, grounding them in their village, their school, their family. Where had that wonderful book gone now? She pictured her creative mother now spending hours upstairs in the attic bedroom, churning out painting after painting. A quiet space for her. Watercolour after oil, oil after watercolour.

Chapter 22

December 1996
Bath

Henry visited San Cassiano in his dreams. The sunlight warmed his soul and coloured the patio where Patience sat on a white metal chair, her bare toes curled around a table leg, reading and sipping a glass of aged Brunello from his cool cellar. She smiled as he came across the flagstones, his feet bare too – no need for well-polished shoes here – and poured himself a glass and sat down to admire her. She pushed a characteristic stray curl behind her ear, her eyes full of love and admiration. She would do anything for him, he knew it; just about anything.

He drained his glass and stood up, held out his hand and pulled her up to him, his hands a soft caress, a learning of her curves and her planes. Her lips dissolved into his. Still holding her hand, he stepped carefully over the uneven stones to the patio doors, and closing them behind them he guided their way upstairs, looking over his shoulder after every other wooden stairstep to embed her smiling image into his memory as she followed behind him.

The door to the bedroom was an entry to another world. A secret, quiet world with long net curtains susurrating in the breeze as they lay on the high-topped four-poster.

There was no room for a husband, a wife or children

in this dream; but it didn't matter. They had faded, been erased from his mind.

December 1996
New South Wales

Australia. Christmas present-opening.

"What on earth is that?" Joe asked.

"Ha ha! It must be a joke present from Matty. Dryer sheets. Mmm, very unusual! She always comes up with some strange ideas, doesn't she?"

"Well, I wish she were here instead."

"Well, sorry. You'll have to make do with me, won't you?" Beth snorted.

"Oh, Beth, we didn't mean it like that. Of course we want you here. It's just not the same without her and the girls, is it?"

Beth sighed. She had spent many hours wandering around exquisite home design stores until she had found the perfect cashmere blanket for her father who had lost so much weight that he felt the cold intensely, shivering if it so much dropped below twenty-eight degrees. Christmas Day was sweltering but Joe was seated in his chair, wrapped snugly, with a smile on his face. She had chosen a heavy hardback book on Margaret Olley, a favourite artist of her mother's; but all they both talked about was Matty's strange gift. If Matty had known, she would have worried that the dryer sheets were in the spotlight. That was not what she wanted at all.

Chapter 23

January 1997

It was around this time that Henry started to phone. Patience felt that receiving letters at a post office box was odd. She had persuaded herself that he was only writing because he was lonely, but perhaps phone calls would be better. No written evidence of anything, untoward or not.

Henry called every Tuesday at 9 am. It was usually the middle of the night for him, but he put Mary to bed, tucking her blankets under and taking her a camomile tea to help her sleep whilst he read the paper and waited for the alarm.

"Good morning, Patience. I hope you're fine. Joe gone to golf?"

Just reminiscing, Patience told herself.

Henry wanted every particular of her day. He rolled the details around until they were smooth and then he popped them in his dream bag ready for use at a later time.

"My life has changed since I contacted you again. I'm so happy, you wouldn't believe it. June can't come around fast enough. I'll wine and dine you; we'll go away for a few days... Where do you fancy? I'd love to take you to Italy but perhaps France if it's only for a few days. What do you think?'

"Woah, Henry. I've only just said that I will meet up with you. I'm not sure about going away anywhere together."

"Oh, please consider it."

"I... I... I'm not sure. If Joe were ever to find out..."

"We promised not to talk about him. That's a different life! This is the one with me!"

And, of course, one day the inevitable occurred.

"Hello, Patience?"

"Who is this? Do you mean Pat?" No one had called her Patience for a long time."

"I'm sorry, I must have the wrong number."

She was quizzed. She had been late coming back from the pharmacy for tablets for Joe and he, not feeling well, had not gone to his regular golf game. She shrugged her shoulders and denied all knowledge of who could have been calling her and addressing her as 'Patience.'

"You've been Pat for so long. I can only think it was a man you knew a long time ago."

"Maybe so. I don't know. Anyway, it doesn't matter. He said it was a wrong number, didn't he?"

Joe had never queried the explanation for the unique piece of Christmas jewellery. When she had shown it to him some weeks later, she had said it had been a golf prize, that she had chosen it with a gift voucher from a competition she had won. She had never taken it off since. Sometimes in the sun the coral glowed, the chain fitting silkily around her neck. Indian skin, still smooth and supple, in perfect contrast to the coral horn. Sometimes Joe would run the chain through his fingers as he lifted it to kiss that unmarked skin. He lifted her hair from her nape; her hands, rubber-gloved in the washing up, flicked up at him. Stop. But the phone call had unnerved him. Since then, he rushed to answer the phone when it rang. He listened in to her conversations. She caught him perusing every piece of post that arrived. He took to loitering behind her as she sat at the desk paying bills and writing airmail letters to Matty. It was disconcerting.

"What is it? D'you feel okay? Why are you standing there like that? I'm writing to Matty."

He was fine, he said, just curious about what took her so long to write.

She told Henry during the next phone call that she still agreed to see him when she came over, but that this telephoning could not go on.

Henry gulped. It was his lifeline: his reason for whistling, his reason to smile. Fourteen weeks was a long time to wait.

Chapter 24

April 1997

Henry began to set things in motion to be available for any of the days that Patience would be in England. He called Matilda as often as he had called her mother until she told him that it was not fair to enmesh her further in this subterfuge. The moral dilemma that she felt intensified with each contact and then faded until the next time. The phone rang; she asked one of the girls to answer stating that she was not in if it was Henry. They found it rather hilarious. Their grandma: who would have thought it?

"It's not funny at all," Matilda answered. "He's becoming a real pest. I don't know what Mum ever saw in him, frankly."

"Well, he does have a house in Italy; could be useful!" the eldest laughed.

Henry had heard from Max that Patience would be in North Wales visiting him and his family. This was an opportunity for him to arrange a trip to friends there. He cajoled Max into organising a tea in Llandudno where he could meet her in the relative anonymity of a tea-room. He thought back to the fly-blown scones in the tea-room in Rhyl all those years ago where he had seen her flirting with another officer. A similar tea-room, cakes in the window, small-flowered teapots on the tables; but a lifetime in between.

He jumped up, almost knocking over the round check-clothed table in his eagerness. He winced as pain ran down his left leg. Patience looked surprised to see a grimaced greeting but smiled and held out her hand.

This would not do. A hand; after all this time. The grip of pain eased him, and he focused on her mouth, the same chipped tooth, the ironic lips. He glimpsed the coral horn at her neck peeking out from a white linen shirt. It was an invitation. He held out his hand and drew her to him. A bridge from the weekend in Bath to the present; wife, husband and children all faded into insignificance. He almost crumpled into the chair as the pain bit him again and he had to withdraw from an embrace he had intended to be soft and romantic.

"Henry, are you okay? You've gone quite grey."

"I'm fine, Patience. Just a bit of old age inconvenience! You, my dear, are looking wonderful."

He superimposed the image of her that he knew so well from the old photo in his wallet onto the person he saw in front of him and found nothing wanting. She was still his smooth-skinned, dark-haired Indian beauty.

"I… I don't have long. Max's son Edwin's picking me up in half an hour to take me on a quick tour of his house in Rowen before we go to dinner at Max and Lucy's. Have you been to their house before? It's wonderful. They've converted an old barn; well, Edwin has. I wish I had a house like that. I love old houses. Joe likes to build new ones."

It didn't matter what she said, whether it made sense or was just prattle; he supped it up, sipped it with his tea and felt the warmth of it in his throat, down into his stomach, until suddenly the heat became emotion behind his eyes, warm and moist. They became red-rimmed and he concentrated on the sugar bowl with its wonky lumps of brown and white sugar; he needed to recover before he could lift his gaze back to the beautiful face. She was not content. He could see that. Her eyes pooling black flashed flinty chips as she asked him about Mary and his daughters – Julia, the younger one, living at home and helping with her mother's care and Fia, working for an international bank in London. He brought her up to date with their love lives, their domiciles, their peeves and grievances as if it were about them they were meeting. A divorced couple, perhaps, updating intimate knowledge of their offspring.

It's strange how two people's concept of time can be so contrary: the same number of minutes to one person passing in a blink and to the other, many more than thirty.

Looking at her watch, she rose.

"Wait, we haven't talked about our few days away. I've booked a ferry, so we can go where we want; what do you think?"

Patience swallowed, looked at the beaky face in front of her, his eyes pleading as he swept his hair back in an age-old gesture. It was that which made her say yes. Say yes, to what would amount to adulterous behaviour, she was sure. Or would it be?

"Separate rooms, Henry, separate rooms. I will call you when I'm back in Devon next week and you can tell me all the details."

Henry hummed for days. He bought some paint and told Julia he thought they should paint Mary's bedroom, freshen it up.

"I found a beautiful apple green; what do you think?"

"Dad, that's not green at all, it's a pale pink! You really should've told the paint mixer that you're colour blind, you know."

"Ha, it's a beautiful colour anyway. When your mum comes back from respite she will love it, I'm sure."

"If I'd known how cheerful you'd be to go away for a few days' holiday, I'd have suggested it earlier."

"Oh, maybe it's just the weather; it'll be good to get away and feel the sunshine."

"Dad, if anything happens to Mum whilst you're away, I will be able to reach you, won't I?"

"Of course! I'm only doing a channel hop, my girl, not going to Timbuktu."

Chapter 25

May 1997

Standing on the deck, looking at the forlorn deckchairs in the blustery Channel wind, Patience leant her arms on the rail, a prop for her indecision, as Henry inched closer. She lifted her arms and shook them, placing them down just a few inches further away from Henry who was looking at her with undiluted desire in his eyes.

Henry had his prize in sight. He could not help but let his need sneak out of himself; it surrounded him as a hazy aura that even the unobservant young girl avidly looking at her phone saw and registered as she glanced up. Her eyes flashed concern at Patience, but Patience was staring out to sea, her thoughts jumbled up like the seawater below. Crashing upon her they filled her with daring and then retreated like waves disappearing into sand on the shore, leaving only a froth of doubt behind.

Henry had no such equivocation. Mary was safe in respite. She had no connection to his spirit, he felt. Mary had abandoned him long ago to draw back into her world where she forever played hopscotch and marbles, fierce determination in her glazed eyes. Until the accident she had been a helpmeet, if not his only true love; she was strong and firm. Besides, she had parents who owned a printing business which helped Henry establish himself. He had not thought that marrying money would have been something he cared about but after the death of his father, his mother had gradually dwindled the family's fortunes to the townhouse in Bath which then became mortgaged and at her death just covered her debts. He had always suspected her extravagance but had had no proof. The death of his sister Martha from an aggressive cancer had precipitated a downward spiral in his mother; and the purchase of every gewgaw or trinket did little to alleviate her mood but merely tinkled or sparkled, momentarily filling her emptiness. Henry was never good enough. She kept telling him so.

"Why couldn't you be a doctor like your father? Why don't you use your brains? You're such a disappointment to me, Henry."

This cry he never could avoid; but he could avoid visiting the rundown home and place the memory of his childhood into a drawer well-hidden. He wouldn't open the drawer unless feeling strong and even then, it was hard to unlock. He had forgotten the combination.

Fifty years of dreaming about Patience had led Henry to this point. It felt like the final step to the pinnacle as he stood beside her, breathing in the sea air and the elusive frangipani note of perfume. Christian Dior, he found out. It made a trip into the duty-free shop mandatory and he presented her with a small bottle.

"This is what I always smell when I think of you. Diorissimo. It is you, really you, that makes it so special."

"Thank you, Henry." She moved closer. "I have always worn this, you know, ever since my father bought it for me as my first perfume! I love it."

Henry put his arm around her waist and pecked her on the cheek, taking the opportunity to breathe in, to breathe her in.

"I can see the Normandy coast over there; we must be getting close," Patience said. "Come on, we'd better go and get our things."

And she walked steadily off, with him limping slightly in tow behind her, his troublesome left hip making him slower.

What he wanted to do and what he would be able to do kept rolling around his mind as they drove to the gite in Bayeux. It was not far in miles but such a distance in years. He had to keep swallowing to stop the rising delight. Patience told him to keep his eyes on the road.

"You're not driving that Singer anymore," she laughed; "slow down and keep your eyes on the road and off me. There, look, you missed the sign! We'll have to turn around now."

He had missed the sign. It was something he often did. He was not the best at reading other people's thoughts or feelings.

That night while getting ready for dinner, he knocked on the adjoining bathroom door.

"Please, can I come in? I just want to see you."

"I'm in the bath, Henry."

"I know. I want to soap your back for you."

It was curious. No one had ever offered to wash her before. No previous lover, no Joe. How could he want to see and touch her old, fading body? Perhaps if she allowed it he would desist from wanting more. Perhaps he would lose his fascination with her. Perhaps it was just the thrill of the chase. Maybe after all these years he just wanted some sort of revenge for her flippant refusal of his affections. Perhaps he would become amorous and she would not be able to fend him off. Amorous?

They were in their eighth decade; who was she kidding?

"Come in, Henry," she sighed.

He stumbled through the door, breathing hard. He wanted this so much but his body was letting him down. His face turned puce as he saw Patience emerging from the bubbles like a Queen of Sheba, he thought. Calm down, breathe slowly.

He dragged the flimsy three-legged bathroom stool close to the bath, sending it strength to bear him.

"I... I just want to touch your skin. I dream of your skin, I dream of its softness, its silkiness..."

He started to caress her back with a bar of soap, her beautiful Indian skin, lathering up and mesmerising himself with the motion.

Suddenly, he wrenched his hand away, as before his eyes her soft Indian skin seemed to be sullied by blood and ripped silk. He breathed loudly, trying to dispel the image, almost snorting, Patience thought. She was horrified. He was old and decrepit. She was disgusted with herself.

"That's enough, Henry. Go away. I can't have this. I've made a mistake. I want to go back to England. Leave me alone."

She grabbed at a towel and pushed him away. He nearly fell off the stool, his mouth gaping open, his dreams swirling like the sloshing bathwater.

Chapter 26

June 1997

"It was a disaster, Matty. I never should have gone. I'm sorry I even considered it. It just felt wrong, you know."

Matty didn't commiserate; she shrugged her shoulders and again wondered how much of this she would tell her sister. She had confided in her about the letter-writing between their mother and Henry, which had horrified Beth; and this, a weekend away, albeit aborted, would cause more admonishments than she felt she could deal with. Henry did not call for the rest of her mother's stay and for this she was grateful. But one morning a few weeks after her mother had flown back, the phone rang just as she was hustling the girls out of the door for the school bus. She picked it up.

"Hello. Just a minute. – Ellie, you've forgotten your lunch box; here it is. – Sorry. Hello. It's Matty."

Her guard had dropped; she had not been expecting the contact. Not now, after what had happened. Her mother said that she felt afraid of him. Afraid of his intentions, afraid of what she was doing.

"Hello, Matty. It's Henry. How are you?"

"I'm sorry, Henry. I can't talk. I think it's best we don't. Please don't call me again."

"But I just wanted to make sure your mother got home safely and that she's okay and that she'll still write to me."

"It's nothing to do with me. You'd better ask her yourself. I don't want to be involved anymore. I'm sorry. I've got to go. Goodbye."

Henry dropped the phone down with a crash. How could this be? He had done nothing wrong.

"I had the best time, Julia," he told his daughter. "Bayeux was magical, all the medieval buildings leaning over the roads; and it was lovely to see it with my old friend. We'll have to do it again sometime soon."

This is what he remembered. He had heard nothing from Patience since she had returned home. He was worried that she might be ill. She had certainly looked wan when he left her at her friend's house in Southampton.

"Don't come in, Henry. Susie's not well, and I told her I'd creep in and not disturb her. Go home, Henry. Go home to your wife."

It had been a strange goodbye, certainly, but not a final goodbye, of that he was sure. He would find a way of speaking to her again. He would.

Chapter 27

December 1997

There was nothing in the news these days, nothing that Henry wished to read about. It was corruption, violence, and death. He shook the paper angrily as he turned to the arts pages. Not even a full spread. He wanted to read a review about a film he had been to see with his next-door neighbour.

Yesterday, Mrs Cherry had knocked on the door with a steak and kidney casserole for him.

"I've brought this for you and Mary," she said. "I thought you might want to go to see Saving Private Ryan on at the Regal."

"Oh, I really couldn't leave Mary; Julia is away this week for work."

"Bob wants to go, and you could go with him. He doesn't like to go on his own and I don't want to see it at all. All that war and fighting stuff, not my cup of tea."

"But Mary…"

"Don't you worry about her. I'll stay with her. We'll have a grand time, won't we, love?"

She chattered on to Mary who stared vacantly out of the window, her life passing in trees, swirling leaves and the occasional pedestrian out walking their dog. Her life ended at the gate onto the road, but whether she saw beyond that, to a life lived in afternoon teas or schoolyard gossip, no one could tell. Her expression changed not a whit. If Henry got frustrated with her and spoke more harshly than warranted, not a muscle flickered. If he stroked her hand or squeezed it between his, pressing his lips in a vain attempt to stimulate, she did not glance or turn her head to gaze into his eyes or even wonder who this stranger might be. Mrs Cherry would talk to her incessantly, and Henry would enjoy his film. He did enjoy it. It was a surprise. He found himself absorbed, for once not thinking of Patience and all she meant to him, but immersed in another story of the war, another life. His war receded.

On the way home Bob persuaded him into the Clarence Hotel for a nightcap.

"So, how are you finding things, Henry? Julia said you managed to snatch a few days away in France earlier in the year. How was that? A real break, I imagine."

Henry twirled his glass, watching the beer bubbles clump and break. He shrugged his shoulders. Bob had been a good neighbour over the years, but their nodding acquaintance and comments about the weather didn't inspire confidences and if he did talk about what was bothering him, he knew that Mrs Cherry (he couldn't think of her as Molly: a barmaid's name if ever there was one) would relish telling tales, "in confidence, you know – poor Henry."

This is what he said: "It was wonderful. Bayeux is a beautiful little town, you know. Do you know that part of Normandy at all?"

'No, can't say as I have wanted to go back to France. The war ruined it for me; once I left that beach I never wanted to return. It was hell."

Henry found himself talking about his time in India, about Peshawar and the incredible carnage he had witnessed in the lead up to and the aftermath of partition. Another hell. An inferno of screams, blood and scarlet slits cut into innocent victims. It felt to him, now, like relating the plot of a film he had once seen, a scene of putrefaction and desecration alleviated only by the lull of visits to the protective shrine of the country club. A haven of British culture and gins and tonics against the backdrop of the lushness of frangipani and soft skin smelling of cinnamon and turmeric. A heady mixture which made him swoon even now, in this dark wood-panelled bar filled with the fug of smoke and warm hops. Dark eyes, flashing a frozen eternity, gazed unseeing at him as the folds of a fuchsia silk sari bordered with gold embroidery spilt across a slender neck. He swallowed his beer and stood up. It was time to go home.

Chapter 28

January 1998

In talking to Bob, he had cracked open a box he had hidden for so long. Padlocks and combination locks sprang apart as image upon image flooded his waking moments. Boiling the kettle, he saw turbanned faces in the steam. He poured them into the bottom of the mugs where they lay hollow-mouthed, screaming. He stirred in sugar and they dissolved.

Later, while walking into town for the paper, the staccato footsteps of running children evoked gunshots. It was only in his dreams that night that he saw the gentle Sunita swaying up the path with her woven basket brimming with golden mangoes. Unsullied and smiling, she raised the sari with her free hand, silver bangles tinkling as they cascaded to her elbow, her gaze aware of his appreciative looks. Her smile was enveloping him, her chipped tooth an endearing quirk as she pushed a stray curl behind her ear. No, wait: two faces swam up to him. Disembodied, they flooded the room, wept into the corners, as he lay immobile in his bed, pinned down by the weight of the blankets; grinning, grinning, the one a palimpsest of the other, moving closer to his face, hovering a foot above, a weight on his chest; suffocating, he was suffocating, a pillow full of memories pushing harder and harder, his breath a tiny wisp. He pushed the blankets off, his chest heaving, his pyjama top clinging to him as he swung his legs off the bed, his feet grounded on the cool wooden floor. He placed his head in his hands, breathing slow and deep until his heart stilled. He slipped his feet into the brown scuffed slippers by the side of the bed, tied the paisley silk belt around the waist of his dressing gown. In the gloom, he spotted the glisten of his spectacles and put them on before wobbling his way down the stairs to the kitchen.

The consoling warmth of camomile steamed between his hands. Days came early, before dawn. He sat by the Aga as the skeleton trees plaited their branches against the yellowing morn. Bleeding pink tinges, he noticed; not a good sign for the day to come. Reflections jumped down off the crystal glasses onto the shelf as the weak sun sliced through the kitchen window, primrose yellow, creating glistening patches on the floor.

September 1998

He walked across to the bay window. He tucked the blue blanket under Mary. It was full of moth holes but Mary in a rare show of emotion had clung onto the blanket when Henry had tried to gently wrest it from her twisted hands. It had been impossible, so the blanket remained, like a child's 'blankie', a dog's chew toy, irreplaceable.

Mary watched russet leaves scurrying around each other with no interest. Henry wondered whether she even saw them.

"It's a lovely time, isn't it, Mary? Just look at those

leaves; we'll hear them crunch under your wheels later. Would you like to go out today? Yes, I'm sure you would. We might even be able to meet Julia for lunch. What d'you think?"

He brushed grey strands off her scalp, pink and tender like a mouse's belly. He whizzed up her daily offering of kale, apple, ginger, orange, and banana, a combination he felt encompassed all the minerals and vitamins she needed.

He sat on the stool beside her. Over time he had changed the height of it as it became harder and harder for him to rise after feeding her. He held the straw to her lips; they were dry and scaly, he noted. He would need to rub in some bee balm later. She supped without changing her focus. Slowly he could follow the track of liquid down her throat; nutrition without soul. Or was he feeding parts of his soul to her, tiny morsels which slipped away forever? He too gazed into the distance.

Chapter 29

January 1977

He told her not to drive. To wait until he got home. Mary had just passed her test and was not the most confident of drivers, coming to it later in life. "The weather forecast isn't good, and you don't need to take those papers to the solicitor today; I can do it when I get back or we can go together tomorrow." In a fit of independence and determination, her decision leavened only in its impact by the absence of the girls in the back seat, she set out along the icy roads. To be fair, it was not her fault. A car coming towards her swerved to avoid a cyclist on the brow of a hill, hit a patch of black ice. Mary swept up the bank to avoid a head-on smash, but the car careened around and flipped several times before coming to rest on its smashed top. Mary's neck was broken. Henry never knew whether she remembered anything about the accident, about her family or her life before. She emerged from a lengthy coma, smiling; he caught her hand gratefully, kissing it until he realised there was no recognition in her eyes, no soft squeeze or even a delicate flutter of fingers. It was all to no avail. He wondered about the day of the crash. Should he have been firm and forbidden her to drive; or, sensing her resolve, should he have come home early to take her or at least be with her in the car? It was easier if he blamed himself.

"Hush, girls, don't cry. Your mother's out of her

coma but I'm not sure she'll recognise you."

May 1999

She didn't. And she doesn't. More than twenty years later Fia swoops in to see how Henry is coping. A salve to her conscience; far too busy with her own life to offer any practical assistance. The house is clean, food is in the cupboard and Julia has it all under control. No need for her to stay. She takes a phone call.

"I have to take this, it's a phone meeting."

Raised voices in the hallway.

"I have to go, Father. I'm sorry I can't stay. Give my love to Julia." She plants a vague kiss on her mother's head. Her shoes march down the stone hallway. Military, Henry thinks, that's where she would have fitted in.

"I thought Fia was coming today?" Julia asks as she closes the front door behind her with a kick of her foot, her arms stretched with heavy shopping bags.

"She had to go back to London. Something important came up."

Julia sighs with no surprise.

"I was thinking about the accident," Henry says.

"Oh, Dad. I wish you wouldn't. You really couldn't have helped it. You know how stubborn Mother was. Come and make me a cup of tea while I put the groceries away."

Julia had not managed to reorganise the cupboards to her liking. It is not her kitchen; it is her father's. Canned goods with labels neatly aligned. Dry goods in date order. Spotless countertops, no fly dirt in the window corners, no cobwebs, a shiny floor which Henry still insists on cleaning nightly by hand. Julia comes down for a glass of water to find him on all fours, a pail of soapy water by his feet. These days his knees ache, and his hip makes crouching impossible; he bends from the waist, but this hurts his back. He will have to stop this habit soon, they both know.

"I wish your mother could drink something hot; you know how she used to love her cuppa. I'm feeling maudlin today, Julia."

"Oh, Dad. Take your tea and sit in the breakfast room, I'll come in a minute. You really should take some more time off. I can look after Mum, I really can. I'm owed a few extra days' holiday. You mentioned you had a friend in Australia. What about going there?"

"I think my long-distance travelling days are over, darling. I think I could go to San Cassiano though, if you don't mind. It's been a while since I saw the old place."

"What a wonderful idea. I know how much you love it. You could stay longer, perhaps, and organise some of that renovation you've been talking about for years."

Chapter 30

July 1999
San Cassiano, Tuscany

He sat in the villa close to the wood-fired stove, a radiant spot in a draughty flag-stoned kitchen. This was not what he wanted. Yes, this was an escape, but he desired more. What was left of his soul ached. He wanted someone to ease it, to take it in hand and gently blow healing warmth into the chill. He knew who that someone was. But how could he even contact her now? He could no longer rely on Matilda; her compass veered in conscience towards her father.

He pulled an old leather attaché case from the bottom drawer of the marble-topped buffet and snapped open the clasps with his forefingers and thumbs.

He had kept them all, like a lovelorn schoolgirl. Neatly bound with a ribbon, every letter Patience had ever written to him. In his hurry to undo the ribbon, the letters, thin slices of pale blue notepaper, cascaded to the floor. He groaned, knowing that the pain would be jagged as he bent over to pick them up. Confused, muddled, he glanced at disconnected sentences.

"Hello, Handsome…"

"I haven't told the folks the details…"

"Quite a spot of talent too…"

"Glad the Kashmir trip was enjoyable…"

Kashmir, 1947

The speeding driver rounded the precipitous bends on the dirt road as he headed up to Kashmir. Henry swung from side to side against the leather seat of the staff car, his heart speculating as to whether he would arrive. He recalled the houseboats on the lake, placid and calm, unfazed by the drama around them. He stayed in one with the silk curtains drawn around him to block the squalid view behind and faced the mountains rising sleepily up from the haze to greet the morning. Steaming chai brought to him on a salver as he woke, chapattis and Kashmiri chicken in the evening. He read avidly and wrote to Patience every day, but she only received one in four of his letters. It made for a disjointed correspondence, but the tenuous thread was not to be broken. He was sure how this would roll out. He remembered. He returned to Peshawar, determined to ask her to marry him, but it didn't work out that way. He remembered his choler at the audacity of Sergeant Edwards wanting to see his Patience, his girl, his future.

He shook his head as another page slipped from his fingers. He was losing his grip.

His cousin Silvia knocked on the door. Without waiting for a reply from the despondent Henry she breezed in. Small and dark, fizzing with energy, she ran the village restaurant.

"Come to eat tonight, Henry, I'm making special pasta. You will like it. Come, I see you are sad. We will make you happy. You come early and talk to Silvia."

Henry smiled up at her. She had teased him

mercilessly as a child, his sombre northern temperament contrasting with her sunny, irrepressible, mischievous one. A bunch of dark curls plonked on her head without any order; his severe haircut of mousy hair inherited from his father as they played jacks together seated on the stone driveway of his mother's family house. Her dusty legs thrust out in front of her as she twisted her tongue in concentration; his skinny ones neatly folded underneath him as he considered his next move.

"Of course, I'll come up at about five if that's all right."

He was not sure that he would spill himself out to Silvia; but perhaps he would. She was the one person, even after the long years of absence – besides Patience of course – to whom he felt he could talk easily and who would listen without judgement.

He looked at his watch. He had time for a walk before going to Silvia's. He put on his walking boots, their toes winking, all mud scraped off ready for their next outing. Shutting the front door, he took a deep breath, his eyes ranging the red-tile-roofed buildings, a neighbour's ginger cat sprawling untidily, the higgledy-piggledy walls delineating the medieval walkways between the stone buildings, some restored, some ruined, others left in varying states of decay.

Running footsteps echoed down the passageways. Henry stepped back, flattened against his front door, hidden from any insurgents who might be running rampant, slashing and slitting any who stood in their way. His face reddened; his breath quickened, ragged in his throat, until he saw a group of five children racing up the road, screaming at each other to run faster. He shook his head, locked the door and climbed the rocky pathway at the back of his house. Steeply he ascended past the vegetable plots, a cornucopia bursting with bright parsley, luscious tomatoes hanging on to drying stems, green beans and purple aubergines, further up under the shade of ripening chestnuts, until panting he stood looking down on the shimmering village, a haze of thyme and marjoram, the cypresses pencil-sharp appearing and disappearing in the heat haze, the mountains behind pleated viridian and forest green.

Clear air: he needed clarity. Rounding the corner of the hill the vista stretched magical beyond him. As a boy, he remembered the goatherds passing, accompanied by clattering bells. Silence: it was hot, too hot. He should not have come so late. Mornings and evenings made the climb easier. His leg ached. A lizard zigzagged across his path as he sat down in the shepherd's hut on the wooden bench facing down the valley. Small clusters of red tiles grouped around twisting roads, tying their inhabitants into an old life, a past life, a good life.

Henry sighed. How would he continue to be in touch with Patience? Colleagues said he was good at solving problems. This problem was no different. A solution would come to him. He unfolded an old newspaper that had been left stuffed in the corner of the hut. Not so old, he thought. He gave it a cursory glance and then started reading a column. It had been sent from a journalist living in London to the local area newspaper of Bagni di Lucca. She talked about her life in London and of her friend living in Bagni.

He stood tall, made more so by his military bearing, shoulders back as if on parade. Brown eyes swept the hills in front as he shifted his weight, wincing to alleviate the pain in his leg. His grey hair, peppered with a few remaining dark streaks, swept back from his broad forehead from what could be called a Roman nose which jutted out, leading him along.

His dark eyes were still clear, but his accurate vision was fading, fading like the cuffs of the well-worn shirt he had rolled up. Loose linen pants: a black leather belt tucked in a few folds around the waist, telling of some weight loss.

Henry had heard of lightbulb moments and this was one. His very being brightened; energy thrummed from his feet to his crown. He could feel his heart pounding at the back of his throat, threatening to burst from under his tongue. This was it. There must be a local newspaper where Patience lived. He would write a column; he would offer local snippets and connect himself to Patience. It would work, he was sure; provincial papers were always looking for free copy. His journalistic qualifications would finally be of use.

Chapter 31

July 1999

On the return from his trek into the mountains he had a leisurely soak in the bath. Ever more certain of his idea he lay back, sweat trickling as he appraised the cool white marble. This had been his first task when he arrived in San Cassiano. A cold mountain house needed hot water and a large bath to soak in after mountain walks. A plumber from Bagni had travelled up the hairpin roads daily for two weeks to tile and replace the bathroom fixtures. Henry was not one for luxury, but a good deep bath was a necessity. He was not going to put up with an old immersion heater any longer.

He smiled as he shaved away any shadow on his face, carefully wiping off the foam, chasing it down the plughole with streams of water from the tap. He remembered how the geyser used to cough and splutter and drops would squeeze from the corroded faucet as he impatiently stood, soap drying on his face. He placed the towel on the rack, squared it neatly, and dressed in cool cream linen trousers, a white cotton shirt and a red silk cravat. Sandals were not an option for Henry. He sat on the bed and pulled up grey socks, his left leg complaining as he hitched it high. He tied the laces on his brogues. His hair smooth, he patted his neck as he sauntered up the flagstone localita. He arrived at Silvia's restaurant just before six o'clock. A few villagers nodded to him as they sat waiting for the feast to begin.

Silvia greeted him warmly.

"Come, cousin, you sit. You see you are not the first here but sit near me, by the kitchen on this bench so you can talk to me."

Henry peered into the wide scullery kitchen, empty but for the long tables spread with freshly made pasta, then glanced back at the trestle tables outside starting to fill with locals and tourists eager to sample Silvia's cuisine. He eased himself onto the bench, his hands clasped in front of him as he waited.

"So, Henry. Tell Silvia what is the matter. But wait, I see you look happier today. What have you done? Your eyes tell me stories. But I don't know what is the ending. Hah?"

Silvia's short fingers moulded the ravioli as she pinched the dough together rapidly, adding another pasta square to the billowing pile on the table. She scurried with a platter of ravioli to the waiting cauldron of boiling water and tipped the pasta in. Pots of aubergines and tomatoes drifted their smells to him. Plates were ferried out to the chatting diners who shouted out their approval amidst glasses of red waved at the bustling waitstaff.

It was not quiet; he had the excuse to keep his tale to himself as he shrugged his shoulders at Silvia and shrank into the busy background.

"Okay, okay." Silvia came up for air half an hour later as the rush started to subside and the waitstaff ran like clockwork as they served the third – or was it the fourth? – course of her extravagant feast.

"Tell me. If you don't want to talk, I'll twist your

arm. You remember?" She threw back her head, red cavern of a mouth echoing his scream as she would twist his arm carefully with one hand one way, one the other, clenching her teeth as the Chinese burn taught him that she would not be beaten at jacks. It was no contest. He felt the pain now and answered unspoken questions. Mary was doing as well as could be expected. He had spoken to Julia the other day and yes, he would be going back to England soon, probably in the next week. No, Fia did not come and see her mother very often; he did not think that she liked any of her family. Yes, maybe Julia would come with him next time if he could find someone to look after Mary; she deserved a break. After all, she had given him some respite to come this time; she was a good girl.

Silvia nodded and shook her head as she should and tut-tutted when needed; and at the end of Henry's updates, she threw her floury arms around him and squeezed any argument out of him.

"You were always a good boy," she said. "Come tomorrow morning for cappuccino. I make your favourite pastry. You come, okay?"

He did. He was not sure if it was the sweetness of the panforte which she made out of season especially for him which enabled the words to flow or whether it was the sense of being in another country, another life, a dislocation from his thoughts and feelings. He might have been talking about someone else as he spilt the story of his love, the love of his life, how he had followed her vicariously all over the world, met and re-met her, how now he was going to need to be very clever to twist the thin thread of connection with others,

163

strengthen it into twine and then a rope to bind them to each other forever.

Silvia listened, her head cocked; she noted the gleam in his eye as he mentioned Patience. She chuckled at the thought of someone so aptly named. All the while her busy hands kneaded the pasta dough and rolled it out, thumping and flattening it into a myriad of shapes.

"I knew when you first brought Mary here that she was not your real love. I saw her nose wrinkle as she stepped through the village, how she shrugged off your hand under her elbow, lifting her foot, you know, like she scared she step in something nasty. Hah!"

It was a picture Henry remembered. He had felt so proud bringing her here, to his mother's place of birth, to his villa. But Mary shrivelled, wrapped her cardigan around her middle, her arms tight around her stomach as she sat on the edge of a chair in the kitchen, huddled around the wood-burning furnace, and asked when they were going home. His sense of pride fell to the floor along with his smile.

In solace he had pulled her close as she lay turned away from him on the old mattress, her knees drawn up to her chest. He stroked her gently, swallowing pride and anxiety. His hand fluttered between her legs and he took her there as she held on to the iron bedstead and made Julia, his sunny daughter: a ripe Tuscan fruit.

That was the only time Mary came to San Cassiano. She was always too busy with the children, too tired even to take a holiday. But Henry knew she hated it, the babel of a language she did not understand, the peculiarity of its old-timeness. Henry had returned on occasion to air the house, to see his relatives and consider his options.

After Mary's accident, he came rarely but now after so many years it still felt a refuge, an island, a life apart.

But it was of Patience he thought. He saw her smiling face as she walked up the stone steps, how she stopped to smell the wild thyme crushed under her sandal, a red toenail against the green. He thought of her lying next to him, turning her dark eyes to his and reading him, reading his every thought.

"I think you should bring this Patience here, Henry. I cook for her. You take her walking. There is still time."

Henry was not sure if there was; his stay here was ending. He felt fevered. The house was not finished. He had less than a week. He stood up, knocking the table.

"I have to see the cabinet maker," he said. "He must make a new kitchen for me. Will you check on him, Silvia, if I'm not here? I must buy a new bed and mattress. It must all be ready," he muttered.

As he kissed Silvia on both cheeks, tiny puffs of flour escaped into the sunbeams, dancing before they fell to the floor. Henry did not notice. He hurried down the path, not even mindful of the flag edges, hazards to his old age, and threw open the door of the house and scrutinised it. A fresh view, he thought; how would she see it? It would need to be a haven, an idyllic space in isolation. She could sit there, on the patio; the windows would need to become doors, thrown open as the mountain breeze whispered down from the hill behind the house. You will never want to leave, you will never leave; stay, stay.

Chapter 32

August 1999

"I think she's missed you," Julia said. "I'm sure she looked at me the other day as if she knew it wasn't you."

Henry sees no flicker, flutter, or shiver of recognition. Mary was Mary. As she always was, cool and unresponsive.

Henry searched for information on newspapers and periodicals in the Mid North Coast of New South Wales. He wrote a piece on his house, his Casa Pazienza, how it was a tranquil space amidst the mayhem of the world, and he sent it to several of the local papers offering copy fortnightly on local issues, events in England and Europe. To his surprise, it was not long before a newspaper contacted him. Yes, they would place his fortnightly column, to be titled From Me to You, and would expect to receive it by email on the Thursday before publication.

"What are you so happy about, Dad? I haven't heard you whistle since I don't know when."

He hummed as he fed Mary. He whistled as he brushed her hair. He felt no pain in his leg. He laughed at the jokes the man at the corner store told him: jokes he had heard repeatedly over the years and listened to with indifference. Certainly, they were not funny, they were often laced with racism or with other dubious content. They took wing and sailed over his laughs, uneven in their flight as they escaped through the front door to land on deaf ears outside.

Henry still had a problem. Patience needed to know that he was going to be writing. Dare he try a phone call and risk Joe answering? Or even worse, to have Patience put the phone down on him? He thought of Matilda. She had been an ally in the early days of his intensified pursuit. No, she had said she wouldn't have anything more to do with being a go-between. But what if he called her and just happened to mention about the column? Surely she would pass on the information; but would she? And how would he know if Patience knew? He yearned to write to her but knew this would countermand the whole subterfuge. No, he would have to call.

"Buy the Mid-Coast Observer. Look for the column 'From Me to You'."

That is all he needed to say.

"You don't normally buy the local rag," Joe said, "unless you're in the golfing results, I suppose. I'll read it when you've finished."

The column's author spoke to his 'friend' in Kempsey; it spoke of his daily life, his thoughts, hopes and ambitions. Seeing it all in print, his declarations, his desires, revitalised that frisson of romance in Patience. She passed over the negative feelings, she chose to forget the uncomfortableness of her short expedition to France, his unctuousness which had made her skin shy. She glossed over the image she had seen hovering behind her in the mirror, the hawklike nose, more so in age, the bowed back and the left leg which often made him list quite heavily. She heard in his words the man in uniform who had come into the bank daily to catch a glimpse of her; the man who waited outside, anxious to capture a glance, a smile or even a frown. She saw once again the tall, stern, handsome if somewhat dour person who now far from being a nuisance and annoying was still holding her gently in his hands, offering caresses and gentleness long gone from her marriage. She glowed with the adoration.

Chapter 33

January 2000
Mid Coast Observer 'From Me to You'

A new millennium. A fresh start to life.
Seated here I watch the night draw in, the skies steel grey as they slide down to cuddle the buildings, to smother any remaining daylight that seeps sadly away. The streetlights, pinpricks of yellow, drop golden plates onto the slick pavements as the homeward-bound workforce huddle down into their winter coats, heads bowed, scarves tight, taut steps to avoid skittering. For me, January is the cruellest month. The glitter and glare of Christmas festivities fade from memory, the bitter months of winter stretch before us. Happily, for me, I can sit in front of my wood-burner and stare into the flames for inspiration, imagining the heat rising off your pathways, the way the oxygen seems sucked out of you as you gasp for fresh air. At least, that is what my friend in Kempsey tells me. She says the heat is often so unbearable that she walks her dog down to the water and stands on the beach, her feet soothed in the cooler sand and water. Even the dog wades in slowly and stands there solemnly, cooling his undercarriage. She says he once tried to roll over, feeling the soft waves over every inch of fur and skin, but like herself did not enjoy the experience of putting head underwater. Hot days and cold days.

I dream, not of Australia – as my experience of it

is only vicarious, through the eyes of my friend – but of Tuscany. Tuscany in the summer, where the hum of insects sings along to the rising heat, where green lizards scurry under my feet as I crush the thyme along the rocky pathways. The mountains shimmer blue, cypresses line the roadways leading into tiny, forgotten villages topped with red-hatted roofs, somnolent in the midday.

Here, days trip over themselves in their hurry to reach the next season; there, days fall back into each other, seamless, medieval life flowing into the modern-day. A heart space, a place for all time, of all time.

It will be February the next time I write. Snowdrops and early daffodils. Our early sunshine. Enjoy your summer.

My dear Henry,

I can't tell you how exciting it is to read your column in our local. It makes me feel warm inside, which in this weather isn't so great, but will be useful in the cooler days of July and August!

To think that you have written these columns for me! I read them again and again. I tell my friends about this wonderful new columnist, although I don't think they see it the way I do, not knowing the circumstances. It would be foolish to divulge as so many of our friends are golfing ones and Joe might easily catch a little of the gossip. Meanwhile, keep writing. It reminds me so much of when we used to write at the end of the war when you were in India. Sadly, as you probably remember, I burnt all your letters in an unsentimental gesture, but now I wish I had kept them.

I have been talking to Matty and she is not coming over this August as planned because of an arts course that Ellie has been invited to attend over the summer holidays. There is a possibility, then, that I might come over to stay with her and the girls for six weeks or so if I can make and freeze enough meals for Joe!

It continues to be so very hot here. I think you will empathise if I tell you it is like India. Relentless heat. I do miss the cooling English breezes and yes, even the rainy, misty days. Do you remember that walk we took the afternoon your mother got cross with me when I didn't go to church? Just you and me striding up the hills of the Combe looking back down on the golden stone of Bath. A perfect town in a perfect vale. I miss that effervescent green of the fields bursting with energy; here, the green is grey; a uniform sleepiness lies over the bush pulsating in its lethargy. Now I sound like I'm writing one of your columns!

Tell me more about Tuscany. A place I have always wished to visit.

Patience

Chapter 34

February 2000
Mid Coast Observer 'From Me to You'

An intimation of spring. Pale primroses smile at me on their soft green rosettes of leaves, limp after a bitter frost. Snowdrops sparkle, their tiny bells fringed with the green of summer to come. Early daffodils and narcissus teased by recent warmer weeks stand to attention surprised into immobility, their hopeful leaves shrivelling brown tips.

Yes, spring is still a fair distance away, but we dream. The crisp air drags the moisture from your lungs and suspends it on your nose tip, nostrils twitching under the moisture-sodden woollen scarf. Venture up the lane behind our house and you tread delicately, ice cracking and snapping in the ruts left by horse and dog. Slithering, you grab for a spare hawthorn branch for support while a robin eyes you, as he flits a few feet in front, crisscrossing the hedges. As the lane winds up the hill, the hedges drop and the vista of the splendour of Bath appears, golden in the low morning sunlight. Visitors flock to see the Roman remains and the pumphouse but here one sees the majesty of the town, neat and complete.

From one golden area to another, thoughts run to Tuscany.

Tuscany in the spring: a glorious birth of life through the dusty remains of winter. Up in the mountains, mist hangs in the valleys, early mornings bitter until the sun rises high and the heat of the day spreads itself buttery over the countryside. Walk the mountain paths now and the oils in the marjoram and thyme rise pungent.

Gregorio's battered van makes its way up around the hairpin bends. I can hear the throb of the old diesel engine, straining to make that last gradient, wooden stringers bouncing and clattering. His job this week is to take out the rotten wooden window at the back of my villa retreat, knock down the wall underneath and replace it with wooden framed glass doors which can be thrown open onto the patio which he will hew out from the rock looming down behind the house. This will be a protected area, cool in the punishing summer months, the rock reflecting cold from its depths.

Escaping the remains of winter, I will travel to my villa next month and will report to you all, still arguing with the summer sun, on my progress. May the ocean and the beach keep you sane.

My dear Henry,
Your column brought back so many memories of winter walks. I still enjoy taking the dog down to the lake, but I find I can't walk so far anymore. The old legs start aching and I think I'm even a little out of breath. A regular puffing billy! But I am sure I could find the energy to walk those thyme-strewn paths you talk about in San Cassiano!

I have decided that I will be coming over in the summer, your summer, and have even gone so far as to book my ticket. I will be staying with Matty and the girls for a few weeks and then go travelling to see Elsie who I'm sure you remember, and Susie my friend from art college. Max might be around, visiting from his Spanish retirement retreat, so I hope to see him too.

I look forward to an update on the villa.

Fond regards,

Patience

March 2000
Mid Coast Observer 'From Me to You'

Spring is officially here. Those shrivelled narcissi have decided to try again and are shooting up marvellously from the brown un-weed-clogged earth. It won't be long: the signals seem to reach weed seeds very quickly, germinating them in every garden bed where they are not desired; cheeky, I think.

In the meantime, I enjoy the display of daffodils planted years ago by my wife. I wave at her from the back lawn as she sits looking at the garden through the window. I am not sure that she sees them, but I hope they bring her pleasure somewhere in her memory. Oh, the vagaries of getting old! My friend in Kempsey was bemoaning the fact that her legs don't work as well as they used to. We all develop minor or major deteriorations as we age, but we still have the capacity to love and enjoy.

Progress on my villa in Tuscany, you ask? A visit is due. Gregorio's work needs surveillance. My cousin tells me that he has removed vanloads of rock from the new patio area but is not sure which way the doors should be hung. Builders, eh? He will need leading by the hand and a longer stay to supervise the new kitchen, I am sure. Next month will bring warmth on the winds. Not warmth like you are experiencing, I know, but we will be happy. Enjoy your slightly cooler days, a portent of your cooler months which of course are not much different to our summer ones!

My friend speaks of all things water. She said that on her last walk to a favourite lake the edges were piled high with foam. It looked as if a manic giant had squeezed a gigantic bottle of dishwashing liquid into it and then set the waves to do their work. The dog was confused and refused to wet his feet as he is accustomed to doing. One hopes it is atmospheric and not pollution driven. So many dreadful stories emerging. However, a pleasing one caught my attention last week, that trawling has been reduced on your Great Barrier Reef Marine Park and fishing reduced by fifteen per cent. Conservation and preservation above all, I say.

More news from Bath and Tuscany in my next column.

April 2000
Mid Coast Observer **'From Me to You'**

Easter, time of rebirth and chocolate eggs! At the back of the Combe, children gather to roll their eggs down the hill. They have spent a few happy hours painting them in every colour under the sun and possibly some new to any palette. My friend in Kempsey tells me how difficult it is to find the right watercolours to depict the Australian skies. I think here she would find inspiration!

There is an annual competition for the most beautiful egg and this year produced a tie. One, painted by a tiny three-year-old, was ablaze like an ovoid Mondrian catching everyone's eye, especially the judges'. Another, painted by a chubby older boy, tousled hair and glasses, looking for all the world like Piggy from Lord of the Flies, had depicted a miniature scene of the view from the hill. So detailed, he must have used an exceedingly fine brush and had more patience than most boys of his age. He stood, scuffed shoes crossed in embarrassment while the prizes were given whereas the three-year-old skipped in excitement waiting to roll her egg down the hill. A sad end to those and other masterpieces, I feel.

A fortnight ago I wended my way to San Cassiano to view the progress on the house. Despite all Gregorio's head-scratching, to me, the opening of the back of the house onto the rock is breathtaking. An influx of light and wind from the hills behind. Common sense for Gregorio had prevailed and the French doors open out onto the patio, the glass reflecting the gleaming grey rock. My cousin huffed and wheezed down the paseo with a small iron table, its curlicues pasted with a patina of many summers. Pride of place. Gregorio puffed sideways on his cigarette and pondered the scene.

"Well," he said, "if I'd known you wanted old, I could've given you two chairs I was throwing out. They were my mother's. Livia went to town and bought two lovely plastic ones, no cleaning, no rust, she says. Hang on, they might still be in my shed. I'll look for you."

The next few days were spent consulting on the kitchen. Modernised but not too modern. Local wood, local stone benchtop, new appliances, all accompanied by much head-shaking. We made progress on this visit but still there will be telephone calls, discussions of colour and cut of stone. There will be surprises; even with my complete understanding of the language, there is always a cultural difference of outlook. Having visited there for all my years and feeling myself part of the village once removed, that removal allows me to stand back, feet firmly planted, and observe. I have spent my life observing; more observations in my next column!

My dearest Henry,

I do so enjoy reading your column and imagining your house in Tuscany. Maybe one day I'll see it? You'll never believe it, but Matty and her new beau are thinking of taking a holiday near Lucca during the time I'm there and have invited me to go with them and the girls. I am not sure if I would be more of a hindrance to them than a help with that handful of a youngest granddaughter, Flick. I suppose it will give them a chance to spend some time together if I babysit in the evenings.

I laughed at your description of the egg-rolling competition. It is many years since I saw one of those. I sometimes look at my paintings and wish I could crumple them up into balls and roll them down a mountain into a crevice! Some days I feel I should give up, as the more contemporary style I've been experimenting with doesn't seem to be bedding in. Whereas before I was winning competitions, I'm now being passed by. At this age, you feel you're always being passed by. For someone who enjoyed attention, it's galling to realise that no one, really no one, pays you any mind! Oh dear, a letter full of grouses and gloomsies just won't do!

The weather has been perfect for me. Nights are gently cool, much better for sleeping so I'm not wandering the house trying to find a breath of wind. Brilliant jewel blue skies during the days with a touch less heat in them make for more comfortable living.

One of the old ducks in the golf revue I'm directing is causing me grief. She thinks she knows better than I and keeps giving suggestions for every bit of choreography or costume decision I make. It's infuriating. Last week I was so tempted to tell her to take over and get on with it.

Joe is not very well. I think he is building himself up in anticipation of my being away! Nothing determined but a vague malaise which manifests itself as needing me at his beck and call all day. He has, however, managed a round of golf this morning, hence the letter-writing today, the day after I read your column.

The dog is stirring after lying flat out in a patch of sun on the deck; he must have heard Joe's car. I'd better go.

Take care of yourself,

Patience

July 2000
Mid Coast Observer 'From Me to You'

Our regular correspondent is on holiday. His column will return next month.

Chapter 35

Henry's eyes fly open at the screech of brakes as the train arrives at the station. His heart beats insistently into the back of his throat, jumping up and down as he tries to swallow to calm himself. He peers through the windscreen as the smoke and screams clear from his mind and familiar cypresses pierce the blue sky.

He scrambles out of the car, brushes down his trousers, smooths his hair and pats the back of his neck. He rolls his shoulders and hurries on to the platform. It would not do to be late; how could he have fallen asleep? He feels that he is failing himself as he reaches towards the pinnacle of his desire. To have climbed so far and stumble on the last ridge.

As he rushes through the barrier he looks towards the last carriage of the train where a figure gingerly steps down onto the platform. She tosses the curls out of her eyes and her head raises to squint up the platform. She is looking for someone. He wants the picture to freeze. His heart squeezes his resolve and shakes him into movement. His Patience. She is coming to him. This is the start of their idyll. He doesn't know if he can survive the reality, sliding pictures of her, her laughter, head thrown back, slim waist, her houndstooth skirt scrunched up as she sat in his father's car, and that skin, that smooth olive skin he replays on his fingers.

The idea of striding and welcoming her with open arms, bunches of lisianthus and sea lavender spilling into her arms, splinters. He drops the flowers as an excruciating pain radiates from his thigh to his toe. She struggles towards him, drags her suitcase, wondering at his hesitancy. He stoops, his mouth open as he fights to bring the tormented leg under control.

"Henry, are you all right? You look so grey," she asks him.

He waves her away, fighting, fighting all the time with the agony. Now? Why now? His brain expands to the edges of his skull, cotton wool to cushion the nerve as the jangling subsides and ache returns. He straightens up, gives her a ghoulish smile and takes a deep breath.

"Patience, my one and only. I'm so sorry. That bloody sciatica. Seems to be getting worse. Here, these are for you." He scoops up the flowers with some of his lost panache and hands them to her, a few of the purple blooms snapped off their stems and dangling.

"I'm so sorry," he says again, "the flowers, they're ruined."

He snaps off the offending stems and throws them over the low hedge, diminishing the bunch.

"Oh Henry, they're fine, it's you I'm worried about. How long has this been happening?"

"I don't want to talk about it, Patience. Here, let me take your case. How was the journey? I hope you're not feeling too dishevelled. It's a hot day; come, let me take you up the mountains and we can sit out on the patio with a cool drink."

"Perhaps I shouldn't have come if you're not well…

I could've stayed with Matty; they're not going back yet."

He stares in horror. Of course he is well. It is unthinkable that she should not be standing here next to him on the platform. The other arrivals have sloped off to their transport, the backpackers have boarded the train; the station is deserted. They stand together as in a film, long-lost lovers, fifty years on. Pictures, photos, images, they all flash through his mind as he puts out a hand for the suitcase and guides her by the elbow, accompanies her, moves her towards his car parked, waiting.

Between them they place the case in the boot; glancing at each other, they smile and then laugh. Tears squeeze out of the corners of Henry's eyes, Patience becomes a blur, a watercolour in his mind. Her blue jacket swirls like the sea. They continue laughing, laughing with embarrassment.

"Look at us," Patience says when she catches her breath, "silly old fools, what were we thinking?"

Henry leans back against the car, a shining dark blue, takes Patience's hands in his and stares at her. He sees the Patience of so many years ago. He cannot see the wrinkles or the loose flesh, the delineators of time and experience; he enjoys looking at the world without his glasses. The glare of the high afternoon sun makes his head swim. Patience squirms as his gaze never leaves her face.

"Come on, Henry." She drops her hands finding skirt material to smooth, her eyes concentrating on invisible specks of dirt on the soft cotton. "Let's go. I want to see this famous house of yours."

Henry hesitates. It is too much. He bursts with desire for her to approve of his villa, to love it as he does. Anxiety smacks his ribs, snaps off pieces and sends them up his gullet, sharp-needled shards piercing his confidence.

"Just give me a few minutes," he prevaricates, "I still feel a little pain. It might be difficult for me to fold myself into the car."

He continues leaning; his left leg bends awkwardly, his weight heavy on his right. Patience shifts from one leg to the other.

"Well, I've been sitting for a while; I'll just take a little wander to stretch my legs if that's okay with you?"

Henry watches her cross the car park. She stands hesitant at the road's edge, but an interesting clump of trees and bushes nestled against the hill beckons her. It borders a gated park, and as she pushes open the protesting metal gate a minute cemetery reveals itself. She fishes in her handbag for her glasses kept cosy in a blue embroidered velvet case to peer at the plaque. She bends down to read the weathered inscriptions on the tombs and gravestones. How strange. An English cemetery here in the mountains of Italy. She struggles to read the mossed and lichened inscriptions. Many stones lean over drunkenly or have been broken into pieces, as though their inhabitants are recovering from an outrageous party. Hungover, they grumble and groan, covered with brambles and overgrown plantings. The small gravel stones, pieces of marble she realises, glint in the path as they lead her towards the tiny chapel.

This is no place for her. She feels fear, fear for herself and Henry as she hurries down the stone steps back through the creaking gate and crosses the road to the waiting Henry.

"You found the cemetery, then?" he says. "I was going to bring you here later. It's rather picturesque, isn't it, and so odd to be here in the backwoods of Tuscany?"

Patience shudders, waves of presentiment washing over her with such force that she cries out as if drowning and takes his hand in hers and squeezes it.

"Come on, let's go," she repeats.

Henry's needle-sharp anxiety lessens but his breathing jags as he drives the car back up to the village. He keeps up a running commentary: bursts of remembrance with every corner they round. The climb elicits short comments from Patience, who relaxes as she takes in the magnificent countryside, the dry dust of summer shaken over the verges and greenery.

Bursting with pride he stops the car next to the villa, and leaving the case in the boot until later, he takes Patience by the hand and ushers her along the stone pathway to the door. He can see on her face that she loves it. She loves the bright flagstoned kitchen, the patio doors open with soft white curtains fluttering in the afternoon breeze. Patience smiles at him and goes outside to sit at the small round metal table. He opens a bottle of wine and he thinks his heart will explode.

Later that day, sitting in the shepherd's hut, gathering their breath as the mist wreathes below them, Henry tells Patience about Sunita. It feels strange to be telling her. It feels as if Sunita is beside him, smiling her shy smile, her dark eyes pools of history, nodding in assent as he explains or thinks he explains how he failed her.

He tells her how he feels confused, how swishes of silken material or touches of soft skin remind him of her, how her shy smile is encapsulated in Patience's own. He stammers as he recounts her death in the marketplace. He says he knows his mind plays tricks; he wakes in the night and holds Sunita in his arms and sees nothing but blackness, a yawning chasm in front of him, a bit like the valley in front of them now. He shakes his head as if to restore himself to this hillside, to Italy, to Patience beside him. The here and now. How he wishes he could be a saviour for Patience, but he fails at that too. She is a prisoner in her life as he is in his. He brushes his eye briskly; Patience stares into the valley.

Henry stands and teeters on the edge of the cliff. In alarm, Patience rushes to him and grabs his hand, pulls him back.

"No!" she says. "That's not the answer."

Chapter 36

October 2000

My dearest Henry,
My life as I see it:

Full of sun-drenched patio days, easel out, watercolours mimicking the mauves and blues of the sky as it drops its velvet folds over the mountains. Carefree, waited on, a glass of wine, soft discussions as the cool evening drapes us.

My life as it is:

Sun-baked days, snatches of painting in between calls for food, help to the bathroom, oh and yes a cup of tea might be nice once I turn away. Where are you? What are you doing? Come and talk to me!

It's a dream, Henry. You of all people know what I mean. You must feel the same. We are two caring people fulfilling our destiny as carers, just not as carers of each other. I feel mean to dream of anything else, wicked to hope that there will be a release. He gets worse.

Cheerio, Henry dear, God bless and look after yourself.

Patience

Henry holds the letter close. As he kisses it, he imagines the soft vellum of her skin. How he wants to caress her and at once feel enfolded both in the giving and receiving of love. He glances across at the impassive Mary seated upright in her chair at the window, blanket grasped tightly in her clawing fingers.

He sighs, checks the time of his doctor's appointment. He doesn't wish for the test results to confirm what he already suspects. So much to put in place for Mary's care. So much responsibility to heap onto Julia. He knows he will never see Patience again. His eyes swim. He suspects he will never return to Tuscany, to his beloved San Cassiano. To his Casa Pazienza. The paperwork on his desk beckons. He stands up stiffly and shuffles over. Last Will and Testament. He scribbles in the margin. Casa Pazienza to be left to Patience Gregory.

Epilogue

July 2001
San Cassiano, Tuscany

The urn sits at Patience's feet, the dying rays of the sun peeping over the top of the mountain making it glint like a dazzling gold tooth. Julia stands outside the hut, leaning against the wall, her shoulders shuddering.

Patience stands, her cheeks now dry as the wind tears the ashes from the proffered urn. Swirling and whirling down the valley. She tips the last of them at her feet where a breeze lathers some onto her damp skin. She cannot wipe them off; they smear smooth and grey. Ashen on her smooth brown skin. A small clunk of a chunk of bone clatters onto a rock and bounces helter-skelter, lost to the depths of the valley. Henry needs no English cemetery to inter his bones. His spirit rises and falls. It will reside here forever.

Acknowledgements

To all those who helped and supported me along this writing journey.

Especially to my writing group who initially thought I should continue and develop the idea; to my family and friends who remained curious about its progress; to my lovely editor Penny Dunscombe who kept me in line and suggested changes which ultimately helped the flow and whose stringent grammatical knowledge ensured me of a grammatically correct manuscript!

I would also like to thank Ross Macleay and Jan Parkin of North Bank Institute of Independent Studies who readied the novel for publication.

And to my early readers, Jessamie Dunton-Rose and Graeme Pauley who offered suggestions and encouragement, with Jessamie setting me finishing goals which were much appreciated.

And last but not least to my mother, without whom this story would never have been written.

Meryl Dunton-Rose is the author of the new novel *A Patient Obsession.* As a teacher and educator for many years Meryl has finally achieved her own goal to write a novel. After completing a BA in Language and Literature Meryl dabbled in creative writing but after completing a Graduate Certificate in Writing she plucked up courage to write seriously with intent! Meryl shares her solar-passive home with her husband, Graeme, and spends time reading, writing, and crocheting in both the beautiful mid-North coast of NSW, Australia and the South West of England where their daughters live (or did so before Covid19 hit!)